Somewhere In The
Far Distance

Manitoba

If you sit alone on a still hot day
Near a riverbank, by a dusty road,
If the air is stirred and you wonder why –
It's the spirit of an Indian passing by.

Isobel King

Somewhere In The Far Distance

By

Isobel King

Published by: Quill
8 Shady Bower Close
Salisbury, SP1 2RQ

First published in 2003

ISBN: 0-9546568-0-6

Printed by:
ProPrint
Riverside Cottages
Old Great North Road
Stibbington
Cambs. PE8 6LR

Acknowledgement

Thank you
to Morag for the photographs
and
Madeline for reading the text.

Dedication

Dedicated to the Native American people I met in Canada

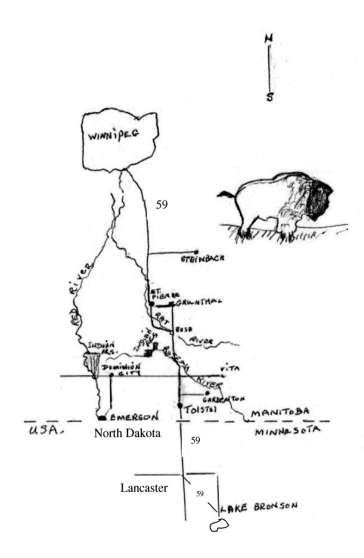

CHAPTER 1

Kathy gazed at the picture in the shop window. A Manitoba farm, the sun shining down on the roofs of the scattered buildings, backed by a clump of Silver Birch trees, the grass stretching away into the distance.

A cold wind blew along the street, but she stood entranced. That was the day that changed her life forever.

She'd just finished her second year at Cardiff University. Her friends had returned to their homes with shouts of, 'See you next term, Kathy.' So also the boyfriend she had tired of. That didn't work anyway, she said to herself as she continued on her way. Not meant to be I guess, like the others before him. Absentmindedly she almost bumped into a pal.

"Hi Kathy, come for a coffee?"

"Hello Jill, I thought you'd left for home."

"Not till tomorrow, I felt too tired. I couldn't get myself together. Stayed too late at the party."

"Okay, I'll come. It seems strange in the city, end of term, no studying to do – Tony's no longer with me. We lost interest in each other. Now I just feel strange. You know how it is, a sort of empty feeling."

Sitting across from each other, Jill sipped her coffee and listened to Kathy with interest.

"At least you drifted apart. Tony didn't dump you."

"No. I liked him a lot for a start, but I didn't like the stuff he dressed up in. I know it's 1970 and all that, but I felt he was a bit of an exhibitionist."

"How did it start, I mean you two pairing off? You didn't seem a likely couple."

"I felt lonely. You know how it is. You feel left out, need a chap to go around with. I've got more serious now somehow. Drifting's not really me. I'm going home later today."

"What will you be doing this holiday?"

"I'm going to Canada," she said with relish, on the spur of the moment, surprising even herself, her brown eyes dancing with laughter.

"Really, I wish I were off somewhere like that, but I've a job lined up. Got to earn some money."

"I've worked every holiday so far. This time I'm doing what I want to do. This Canada thing has been building up in me for some time. Now it's take off time."

"Maybe I'll manage something myself next year."

"Why not Jill? I know I'd be bored if I went back home for another holiday, working for Mum and Dad in our hotel, down in Torquay."

"How are you going to manage for money? It'll cost a bit."

"I'll buy a Student's Travel Ticket. Might as well see some of the world. I've always wanted to go to Canada. I've some relations in Winnipeg. I can go to see them. Manitoba is a good place to explore."

"Well I hope you have a great time Kathy. I'll look forward to hearing all about it when you come back," she said, a little enviously.

"Thanks Jill," Kathy said, getting up from her seat. "I want to branch out on my own." She stuffed her long black curly hair inside her coat collar, pulled back her shoulders, a determined look on her small oval face. "Bye now."

"Well Kathy you've surprised me. I wish the weather would improve. It doesn't seem like June."

"It can be hot in Canada in July. I can kid myself I'm working too. You see there's a lot of wild animals in Manitoba. Just the place for a zoology student like me."

Now that she'd made her decision, the excitement of it all began to take hold. Dad will be pleased I'm going. He always wanted to go to see his folks himself, but time just went on passing by and somehow or other he didn't get around to it, she thought.

On the train to Torquay she began to make her plans. She took a letter from her bag that she'd received a few days earlier from her aunt Amy in Winnipeg. She seems a lovely person, Kathy thought. How sweet of her to suggest I go there. I'll phone her tonight and arrange the date of my visit.

The train sped through the countryside. She sat and dreamed what would it really be like over there. Four weeks of adventure. I wonder where my impulse will lead me.

CHAPTER 2

On a quiet, tree-lined street in Winnipeg, behind a white picket fence, stood a little white painted, wooden house. There on a hot afternoon in August 1970, Kathy Roberts arrived to visit her aunt Amy and uncle Bob. Amy, seeing her from a window, hurriedly made for the front door to welcome her. A little tabby cat, ran purring out and peeped at Kathy from behind a pot of bright-red fuchsia on the doorstep.

"Come in Kathy," her aunt cried, giving her a hug and a kiss, a gleam of delight spreading across her pleasant face.

"I'm so pleased to be here at last Auntie," Kathy replied, putting her case down in the hall.

Half exuberant, half anxious, Amy ushered her into the cool little sitting-room, where partially drawn blinds of green canvas kept out the bright sunlight.

"Bob, Kathy's here," Amy called excitedly to her husband.

A tall man with balding grey hair, came towards Kathy with outstretched arms. "So this is my niece Kathy," he said, folding her in his arms to kiss her.

"Now," Amy said, "have a seat dear and I'll get you a cup of tea. I know English people like tea, but you can have coffee if you like."

"Tea will be fine thank you."

"Did you have a good trip over?" Bob asked anxiously. "Do you like to fly?"

"Yes, great trip, no problems."

Amy came back with tea and handed Kathy a cup. "Make yourself at home dear."

"I feel as if I'm dreaming, now I'm here," Kathy said leaning back in her chair and drinking her comforting cup of hot tea. She had felt rather apprehensive about coming to Canada.

"I reckon it was rather difficult for you to decide to come so far by yourself," Amy said generously persuading her niece to eat something. Her blue eyes pondering, she looked across at Bob. "We've been so looking forward to seeing you," she said admiringly.

"We sure have. How's your mum and dad?"

"Oh! fine. Always very busy you know. That's fine, a hotel with hardly any visitors would be no good. I've helped Mum and Dad the

3

last two years. Being a student I needed a holiday job, but this year I made up my mind to travel and it had to be Canada."

Bob paused, he was remembering his much-loved elder brother. "I always thought your dad would come back here sometime," he said quietly, a wistful expression on his tanned face.

"I think there've been times when he wanted to come, but he's happy back home in Devon. I grew up thinking Canada a magical place. He used to tell us exciting stories when we were little, about life on the farm over in Saskatchewan. I'm fond of the song Dad sometimes sings, 'Farewell to the Red River Valley.' To me it conjured up so many lovely things about Canada and now here I am."

"Yes," Bob said, "I also like that song."

"As kids we played on the buffalo skin Dad brought with him from Canada," Kathy continued. "Maybe he thought he was taking a bit of Canada with him when he left. Anyway we thought we were a race apart, the other children didn't have a buffalo skin to play on."

Bob looked at his niece, a beautiful, spirited girl of twenty, full of enthusiasm and became imbued with her keenness. His wife too, found her niece's happiness infectious.

"I want to learn all I can about Canada and its wildlife. I want to take photos too," Kathy explained, pushing back her black curly hair from her face, her brown eyes shining.

"I can understand you wanting to, as you're a zoology student," Amy said.

Feeling more at ease, Kathy continued. "I'd like to go to some museums and a library before I set off to explore."

"A good idea. We have some fine stores too, in Winnipeg. The Hudson's Bay is one of the best. They've a display there, of things the Indians and Eskimos have made."

Kathy was touched by her aunt's eagerness. "I'll love seeing it all. Thank you Auntie."

Meanwhile, Bob was dipping into a small cardboard box, full of old dog-eared, black and white photographs. "Here are a few photos I've looked out for you to see, they're all family ones."

"Oh good, I'm working on a Family Tree," Kathy exclaimed, "and I want to find out as much information about the family as I can."

Some of the photos she had seen before, but many were new to her. There was one taken, she thought, sometime in the thirties, which puzzled her. Holding it out she asked, "Uncle Bob, who is this?"

Bob took it. "That's your great-aunt Ida, a sister of your grandmother. She lost touch with the family when she married a farmer and went to live in Southeastern Manitoba some years ago."

"I think she's a bit like me," Kathy said, looking more closely at her. Then an idea occurred to her. "When I go down there I'd like to find her if I can."

"If you want to do that, keep the photo meantime, you may find someone who remembers Ida."

"Thanks," Kathy said, popping the photo into her handbag. "I'll try anyway."

Bob had more photos to show her. "These may interest you, they were taken at Fort Carlton, Saskatchewan, near where your gran and grandad lived."

Kathy gazed at them. "How wonderful, Indians, in traditional dress, feathered head-dresses too. I'd be thrilled to see something like that."

"They were taken in 1936, at the time of the celebrations for the sixty years of peace and the signing of the Peace Treaty with the Indians. There's Lord Tweedsmuir, the then Governor General of Canada, being made an Indian Chief for the day."

"It was all pretty violent in the past though, wasn't it?" Kathy said sadly.

"Not something we're proud of," Bob added, "but the government today has a very different attitude towards the Native Americans."

"Good," she replied emphatically. "Thanks for showing me all those photos, they were just what I wanted to see."

A week later, Kathy was shopping by herself in the Hudson's Bay store for presents to take home. She looked longingly at a gorgeous Native American feathered head-dress and wished she could buy it, but it cost far too much. However, she had bought a small replica of an Indian drum for her brother and a little wigwam with a Native American woman standing at the entrance, for her mother. She had also bought, for her father, a pale yellow, fringed

5

leather notecase. A Native American Indian, wearing a splendid feathered head-dress, was painstakingly branded on the front of it.

As she held it in her hand, she remembered Longfellow's poem of 'Hiawatha', she'd read at school and the poem took on a whole new meaning for her. So when she walked out onto Portage Avenue, the main shopping street, to face a stream of oncoming pedestrians, in hot sunshine, she decided it was time for her to leave Winnipeg and discover the real Canada. Tomorrow, she told herself, I'll go to see the prairie, the bush, the rivers, the wildlife and so much more. I might, with a bit of luck even find Aunt Ida.

CHAPTER 3

Kathy hired a car and with a feeling of anticipation, drove out of the city and onto the fifty-nine highway going south. She felt she was on the threshold of a new dimension and it all lay stretched out before her.

Though it was only ten a.m., the day had every indication of being very hot. There were little heat waves, mirages on the road that from a distance, looked like stretches of water, but that disappeared when a few feet away from the car.

She drove along, feeling the sweetness of success. At last she'd arrived, after all her planning and effort. I'm so lucky, she thought and I'm going to make the most of it.

The landscape around was wide open farmland, with a few farms dotted about. Noticeable were the big wooden Dutch type barns, mostly painted bright red. All seemed so peaceful, the long straight road, not much in the way of traffic and the great expanse of blue sky that made everything look so very small. She noticed the little houses along the way had net-screen doors and windows fitted, to keep out mosquitoes, flies and other insects.

A few miles along the road she came to the small town of St. Pierre, with its nicely spaced little houses, mown grass and trees, like a small oasis, she thought. She stopped the car at a roadside café, thinking it would be good to get out of the hot sun and have a cold drink. With relief she stepped into the shade of a green awning and entered the little diner. Making her way to the counter she asked for a milkshake, then looking neither to right nor left she sat down at an empty table.

Kathy was considering the next part of the journey when she became aware of two men sitting at the next table, listening to one in particular, as she was struck by his very pleasant mellow voice. Glancing round, she saw they were Native American Indians, though they wore shirts and jeans much like her own.

Turning her head slightly to see the one speaking, she was surprised to find herself looking straight into the remarkable brown eyes of the young man with the attractive voice. He held her gaze, as she regarded him with honest appreciation. She looked quickly down, hoping he hadn't thought her rude. She'd been surprised to see them there. Now she was embarrassed, feeling she hadn't handled the situation very well.

He spotted her camera on the table. "Have you taken many photos?" he asked quietly.

Partly from relief that she hadn't offended him and of a desire to speak to him, she said brightly, "No not yet. I only brought it in as I thought it might be stolen if I left it in the car."

"Sure it could. Do you want to take photos of anything in particular?"

"Places with atmosphere. I'm on holiday from England and I want to see all I can of this part of Manitoba."

"England'll be a bit different from round here I reckon."

She started to laugh and began to feel better. "I'll say it is," she said and then fell silent. She wanted so much to keep him talking, but she felt she might say the wrong thing.

She looked up when he asked, "Where you heading for?" His expression was one of friendly interest.

"I want to see the bush and maybe some wildlife. I'm a zoology student. I've just arrived here, but I'm really interested and want to make the most of my visit."

"I'm into wildlife and conservation myself," he said. "I'm Albert, this is John," he explained, indicating his companion.

"His name is Albert Thunder," John said. "Don't you think it suits him down to the ground?"

"I don't know," she replied, looking thoughtfully at Albert, he had a gentleness about him, she found attractive. Her mind seemed to be whirling round, but then with sincerity she said, "I think it's a nice name."

"What's your name?" Albert asked.

"I'm sorry, didn't I say? It's Kathy Roberts."

He nodded, "I reckon that suits you too."

She'd finished her drink and began to hesitate about leaving. She really wanted to stay and chat, but thought she'd better go.

"You're off then?" John asked.

"Yes it's been nice talking to you."

"Have a good holiday," Albert said. "Maybe we'll see you around."

"Yes maybe," she replied, going to the counter. There she bought two bottles of Canada Dry and a honey melon before going out.

8

Settling herself in the car, she put the radio on and drove off, thinking about her chance encounter with the two Native Americans, and of Albert's long black hair and friendly smile. The radio station at St. Paul Minnesota was playing western songs, and Merle Haggard was singing 'On the Road' which Kathy thought very appropriate. The further south she went the more wooded the countryside became, with clumps of trees and bright red berries in the undergrowth. Kathy hadn't really known what to expect, as in Winnipeg the city people called the bush, the sticks.

She saw a road sign pointing to Roseau and remembered seeing Roseau River Indian Reserve marked on the map. Sometimes she caught sight of a small animal, a chipmunk or a skunk and wondered if she'd see a deer or other large animal roaming about.

Just past a roadside garage she saw a sign to Dominion City, really only a small country town. There was a possibility someone might have seen or heard of Aunt Ida, she thought, so she decided to go there.

Her uncle Bob had told her that German Mennonites, Germans and Ukrainians lived in the area, but she'd hardly seen anyone about and seemed to have the whole place to herself. Dust blew up in a cloud behind her car as the tyres crunched along the grit road. There were fields of alfalfa, a cattle food and various other crops to her left. Acres of sugar beet and grass soaked up the hot sun.

Some distance further on she stopped to photograph a huge field ablaze with gold and brown sunflowers, to Kathy a really spectacular sight. When she tried to start the car again nothing happened. After several attempts, with only a rattle response, she unhappily accepted the fact that the engine was not going to start and that she was stuck at the side of the road with the temperature soaring into the nineties. Getting hotter and hotter by the minute, Kathy was thankful to see a small red truck coming towards her in a cloud of dust.

She decided to get out of the car and stop the driver, with the hope of being offered some help. A sunburned young man, about her own age, wearing a wide-brimmed straw hat over a mop of bright fair hair, ground the truck to a halt and sat grinning at her.

"If it's car trouble I might be able to help."

"Yes, it's car trouble. When I stopped just now to take some photos it wouldn't start again. It's a hired car, I only picked it up this morning. I hope you can help."

"I reckon I could always try to help an English girl. If not I can sure give you a tow to the garage on the highway."

Kathy felt disappointed as she watched him inspect the engine. Things had started so well, but perhaps it's only a small problem and easily sorted out, she thought.

The young man shook his head. "I can't fix that," he said, and unhappily Kathy found herself being unceremoniously towed back along the grit road to the garage.

"Come back later. I can't look at it just now. I have some farm machinery to see to first, that's wanted for harvesting. I'm sorry Jake to keep you hanging about. I'll get the young lady's car started on after that," they were told.

"Right Dug," Jake said, "we'll call later."

Kathy stood wondering what to do, then Jake said, "I'm Jake, what's your name?"

"Kathy Roberts."

"I guess you could come home with me if you like. I'm on my way there for lunch. I've got younger brothers and sisters, they love visitors."

Kathy hesitated, then she said, "Well, that's probably the best thing for me to do. Thanks, I'll do that." So she climbed aboard the red truck.

In no time they were turning down a farm road and several dogs of various sizes, types and colours, all barking madly, sped up to meet the truck, followed by half a dozen barefoot children. They all ran with the truck till they arrived back in the yard. How some of them didn't get run over, Kathy didn't know. Cats, dogs and hens scattered in all directions as she found herself propelled on a tide of small children, towards the metal screen door of a large wooden shack. The screen door clanged shut behind them and Kathy found herself in a crowded farm kitchen.

"Mum, look who Jake's brought home," one child cried.

Her mother turned round from a large wood-stove, where she was stirring the contents of an enormous cooking pot.

"You guys stop all talking at once," she ordered. Pulling a chair out from under the table, she dusted it off with her apron. "Here sit down," she commanded, "before you're knocked down in the fuss."

Jake introduced her and explained what had happened.

"I'm Hilda. These are not all my kids. Some are my sister's, come over for the day. Bad luck your car breaking down."

"I'm glad to have somewhere to go for a little while. I'm from England on a visit."

"Glad Jake brought you home," Hilda said. "Stay and eat with us. Here's Dad now."

A big, broad shouldered man in working clothes came in and threw his straw hat into an armchair. "Hi there," he said, giving Kathy a big smile, "we've a visitor then."

"This is Kathy," Hilda told him. "Her car broke down. It's over at Dug's garage getting sorted. She's from England."

"Nice to see you. I'm Walter."

"I was on my way to Dominion City," Kathy explained. "Jake stopped to see if he could fix my car, but he couldn't and he had to give me a tow to the garage."

"Course he should," Walter said, "he sure couldn't leave you at the roadside."

"It's so hot out there," Kathy replied, "and good of you to take me in."

"Go and get yourselves cleaned up at the pump," Hilda ordered the children, "and hurry, we're waiting to eat."

When they were all finally seated, Walter said grace and then everyone started talking at once.

"This is bortsh, Ukrainian beetroot soup, would you like some Kathy?" Hilda asked.

"Pass the bread," Walter said, as he tried to get things organized.

"What lovely bread. Do you bake it yourself Hilda?" Kathy asked.

"I bake bread every morning. I've got to, with this lot to feed."

Kathy thought what a daunting task the mother had to face every day.

"We've eight children," Hilda explained, "and love them all."

The children sat in a line on a bench and were all trying to talk at once. Kathy felt like a queen with all the attention heaped upon her.

Walter turned to her, "If your car isn't ready when Jake takes you back to the garage this afternoon, he can take you to Dominion City, if that's where you want to go."

Jake nodded, "Sure I'll take you there."

"I was on my way there to see if I could trace an aunt of mine who married a farmer just after the First World War. We have no trace of her since that time."

"Most of the English people live over by the Red River," Walter replied, "Emerson way you know."

"I want to see the Red River," Kathy remarked.

"Are you going fishing then?" Jake asked.

"Course she's not going fishing. Don't be daft," Walter retorted. "If there's any fish in it you can't eat it."

"Why, what's happened?" Kathy asked, with consternation.

"Mercury in the water," Hilda said. "It's the American factories that cause the problem. They are supposed to be cleaning the river up, but guess it'll take a long time."

Kathy considered what was said. "Of course, the river runs from America up to Lake Winnipeg. I saw the floodway there, last week. It was constructed after the Winnipeg floods of the 1950s, wasn't it?"

"That's for sure and it flows up from America where it thaws first in spring and it's still frozen here. That's a problem. Sometimes the ice builds up so thick it has to be blown up with dynamite before the water can flow up to Lake Winnipeg," Walter explained.

"It causes floods when the river overflows," said Hilda.

"I saw a sign to Roseau on my way here. There's a river there, I'd like to see."

"Indians live there on a reserve," Jake said. "They'll scalp you if you go there."

"Don't be stupid," retorted Hilda. "Fancy saying a thing like that to the poor girl."

Jake's little sister Mary chimed in saying, "When it's dark, Indians come and look in your windows. You have to shut the curtains so they can't see in, Jake said so."

"Don't be daft," scolded Hilda. "He's only teasing you."

"The Indians keep very much to themselves." Walter pointed out. "We don't see much of them. There's times they come here when they run out of gas on their way home from a hunting trip, but anyone can do that. It's a fact people must help anyone stranded in a car in winter. The temperature can be thirty or forty below and folks could freeze to death in no time."

"If you help the Indians they come back with the money or something they've made," Hilda said. "They don't ask anything from a woman, they always ask for the man of the house."

Kathy listened to all the stories, but didn't say anything about Albert. They seem to have a very bigoted view of the Native Americans she thought.

"Do you have many wild animals round here?" she asked.

"Plenty I reckon," Walter replied. "Coyotes, black bears, sometimes moose, bobcats, deer and timber-wolves. There are one or two lynx and cougars, not many."

Hilda told of how little Danny had come running in the week before to tell her there was a big brown horse in the field with the horses. He was so excited I went out to see what it was he'd seen and there was a big male moose standing looking at us. Fortunately it trotted off into the bush. Some of our neighbours phoned the conservation officer to report seeing it."

The meal was finished and Abe, Danny's older brother said, "We have bones in our bush, come and see Kathy."

She was helping to clear away and Jake and his father were sitting drinking a can of beer.

Kathy looked enquiringly at Hilda. "Sure," she said, "go and look. Jake'll be ready shortly."

So Kathy was escorted along a little track in the bush, then Abe stopped. A few steps off the track he showed her some large dried, pitted bones. She bent down and picked one up. "Do you know what these are?" she asked.

"No."

"Well they're buffalo bones. I've seen them in a museum. Maybe some wolves killed it and had it for dinner a long time ago. You could take them to a museum if you wanted to. Have you seen any buffalos?"

"No there's none left."

"Yes, there's parks for them to stay in, where people can't shoot them. Maybe you'll see some one day."

They went back to the yard. Jake was outside fooling around with the children, who were all laughing and shouting. Hilda was sitting out on the wooden steps of the porch and Kathy sat down beside her. Jake was throwing sunflower seeds at the children to catch. The seeds and shells were sticking in their hair and going

13

down their necks. There were yells of pain as bare feet stepped on sharp shells. Kathy ducked to avoid some seeds thrown at her. The children stuffed seeds into their mouths and spat out the shells, the dogs joining in the fun. Finally the children ran off to play another game.

Jake jumped into the truck. Kathy said, "Goodbye," saying she would send a card from England when she got back home.

As Jake drove away, Kathy looked back at the farm and thought how snug it was, but she thought too of the cold winter. There was the pump by the well, the towering stack of straw bales by the big red barn, the wooden shack, home for the family and the odd assortment of sheds and the granary, all sheltering the yard.

A little clapboard house stood by the farm track. "Mum and Dad lived in that house when they were first married. Now it's the hen house. We kill all the chickens before the winter, too many predators and too cold."

CHAPTER 4

As Kathy half expected, her car was not ready when they arrived back at the garage.

"It'll be ready I guess about five o'clock," Dug said.

"I figured that," Jake said to Kathy. "I guess you'll come to Dominion City with me then. I'll bring you back when I go home at four-thirty."

"Fine, thanks very much. I'll take the melon and drinks out of the car, but I'll leave my case in the boot. We might need these," she said putting the drinks and melon into the truck.

Jake started off once more along the grit road. When they met other trucks and cars they had to close the windows to keep out the clouds of dust sent up when they passed by. It obscured the road for some yards ahead, covered the truck, got into their hair and on their clothes.

"I suppose people just get used to it," Kathy remarked, a bit mystified by it all.

"I guess it's what you make of it. The girls don't like it in their hair, it makes it kind'a tough. The gritter comes along in the mornings, the machine for levelling the surface of the road and then it's sprayed with water. The sun soon dries it though and it's back to ruts and bumps again. I guess you don't have grit roads in England then?"

"No, most are tarmac. Look at all the little bugs and grasshoppers on the windscreen," she said, "I haven't seen some of these before. What enormous grasshoppers. Look at that big floppy river fly."

"You'll sure get plenty of them in the evening," mocked Jake, while smartly taking the big insect off the windscreen and sticking it into her hair.

Squealing she grabbed at her hair. "You nasty thing," she shouted, slapping his arm.

"I could sure get a bit rougher," he grinned meaningfully.

"Oh thanks," Kathy said, then thought it was time to calm things down. When she saw an old abandoned farm in a clearing, not far off the road, she asked, "Would you mind stopping here please?"

"What you wanna stop here for?" he drawled.

"I'd like to take a few photos of that farm."

"Okay," he laughed and swinging off the road, he drove with a bump into a dried up ditch.

"Well I reckon I'll leave the truck here," he said, hoping to provoke her and get his fun out of it.

"I'll take out the melon and drinks, it's so hot in the truck." Quietly she remarked, "We could sit up there where it's cool, for a short time, okay?"

They walked the short distance up the farm track, in silence. Kathy stood looking about her at the dilapidated farm buildings and the corral's mossy wooden fencing posts.

"Isn't this a magical place?" she whispered.

"You girls, you're always looking for magic castles and men on white horses."

"I'd hardly call you a man on a white horse."

"Where'd you put the drinks?" he asked rudely.

"Here," Kathy said, handing him a bottle, "I'll just snap a few photos of the corral and the stable. I won't be long." She hung her shopping bag and handbag on a nail just inside the stable, before taking the photos she wanted outside. The old neglected wooden buildings created just the atmosphere she was looking for. Then looking around inside the corral she found what she thought were large oblong nuts, like pecan nuts, the colour of conkers. Taking them over to Jake, she asked, "What are these?"

"They're baby moose droppings," he said. "You want to watch out, maybe a mother moose will come charging out of the bush after you."

"Don't be daft," she said looking round. "The people who lived here before must have left some time ago." Sitting down by Jake, she took the cap off a drink bottle. "I wonder why they left?" she asked.

"A bush fire I guess, there are permanent fires underground around here. They smoulder and break out any time in hot weather. One could break out now and your hair would catch fire, you'd need me then to put it out, so don't be so clever with me." He nudged her playfully.

She moved away from him to the stable.

"See here," he called, "here's some mushrooms. My mum cooks with these." He put a piece in his mouth. "Try a bit."

"I'm not eating it."

"How come? It's tasty," he said, cramming a bit into her mouth as she ran into the stable to get out of his way. She started choking and swallowed it. "You idiot," she shouted, "I'm getting out of here," realising too late, it was the wrong thing to have said, Jake had slammed the door shut.

"Now you're my prisoner," he said, grinning at her through a small gap in the wooden door, before going off laughing.

"Come on," Kathy called. "I don't think it's funny. Let me out." She banged on the door.

He came back to stare at her through the gap. "Are you getting mad with me? You've got to stay there, you need to be tamed a bit."

"Don't be stupid, let me out."

"Don't be stupid," he mocked. "I'm going to the shop for another cold drink. I figure you'll cool down a bit in there."

"Jake," she called loudly, but there was no answer, he had gone.

Well I'm not going to panic, she told herself, that's what he wants. She looked around to see if there was any way out, but it was a very secure stable, only cracks and chinks between the wood planks where sunlight filtered in and made curious patterns on the floor.

Seeing some straw lying in a corner, she sat down and prepared to wait. Perhaps, she thought, young lovers come in to spend some time alone. I hope Jake's not gone long, she thought anxiously. At least it was cool inside.

She had a headache and felt sick. Going over to an old drain, she was violently sick. She crept back to the straw and lay down. Feeling very tired, she fell asleep.

It was evening when Kathy woke up. The last rays of the sun had painted a brilliant golden sunset in the sky when she looked through the gap in the door. Jake hadn't come back. The mushroom had made her sick, she supposed, so Jake would therefore be sick too. Probably no one knew where she was.

She looked around again and found a brown clay pot in a corner. In it she saw a little starved mouse. "Poor little mouse," she said taking it out. It hadn't been dead long by the look of it. She examined its fur and little pink ears, "to die in the middle of plenty at harvest time." Perhaps, she thought, if nobody finds me I may suffer the same fate. She put the little dead creature back in the jar in the corner and lay down again, her heart pounding, would Jake come for her? As the night-birds were calling in the trees and crickets chirped in the grass, she fell asleep again.

CHAPTER 5

The following morning Kathy woke with a start. It was just getting light and for a minute she couldn't remember where she was. Hail was rattling down on the roof and a big clap of thunder reverberated on the ground. Slowly it dawned on her where she was and that she'd been ill.

The storm intensified. Kathy got up and on wobbly legs went over to the door to look out. Through the gap she could see a bit of the bush and the remains of an old John Deer tractor. The flashes of lightning lit up the sky. To Kathy, who had not experienced a prairie thunderstorm, it was awesome. Blue lightning flashed on and off like neon lights and the thunder's continuous roar sounded like a train in a tunnel.

After some time the wind died down and the storm abated somewhat, but the occasional flash of blue lightning revealed an animal standing by the tractor. She could tell it was a large animal, something the size of a German Shepherd dog. Its ears seemed to be on a level with the top of the old tractor's tyres. She took a closer look and to her amazement saw it was a timber-wolf. With each flash she could see it quite clearly as it remained in the same spot, staring in her direction. Kathy knew it was aware of her presence, but after a few minutes it trotted off. Hardly able to believe what she had seen, she took the melon out of the bag, went back to the straw and sat down. She couldn't eat it however, but she had a drink.

She was now feeling much better. When she looked out again she saw a woman and child some distance away, picking bright red crab-apples. She called to them several times, but they didn't hear her. After the storm everything was sparkling in the sunlight. The dust had settled, grasshoppers were everywhere, chipmunks ran between the bushes and a persistent woodpecker drummed on an nearby tree.

Kathy stayed by the door a long time, hoping to hear or see someone about, but no one came near. She dreaded another night alone.

She remembered that while she slept she had a dream. An old Indian woman stood over her, concerned for her. Kathy could distinctly remember her long embroidered Indian dress and sewn deer-skin shoes.

It was late in the afternoon when Kathy saw a spiral of smoke not far away and wondered what it was. She watched it for a few minutes as it rose thicker into the air and hoped it wasn't a bushfire out of control.

A reddish glow crept across the sky and huge clouds of black smoke started billowing upwards. An ominous pall of smoke soon hung over the bush. Kathy knew that if the fire came her way she would be trapped in a deadly situation.

Now smoke began to drift through the nearest trees and in the eerie half-light a sense of helplessness overwhelmed her. The firefront was widening rapidly by the minute from the look of the smoke. A few animals began to appear at the edge of the bush. Two skunks ran out. She could now hear the crackling of the fire and birds were gliding from the trees.

Calling loudly, "Help, help," she began trembling with fear.

The yard began to fill with smoke. Soon she would be unable to see out. The smoke was making her cough and she was shaking all over.

Suddenly a man ran quickly into the yard and Kathy thinking he was going past shouted, "Help me, please help." He stopped and then ran forward. To Kathy's relief the door sprang open. She grabbed her camera and dashed out, to be confronted by Albert.

For a brief moment they stood looking at one another with astonishment, then Albert took her camera and stuffed it into his pocket.

"Oh boy! What have we here?" he asked, taking her by the hand. "Hurry," he said pulling her along as fast as she could go. "We'll make for the River Roseau, it's not far away, then we'll be safe."

Her eyes were stinging. She struggled to keep going, with him still holding on to her hand to keep her from slipping. All she could think about was, would they be able to get away from the crackling fire?

"Just a bit further," he urged her reassuringly, as she struggled for breath. Little animals were running here, there and everywhere. Kathy felt so sorry for them. She almost fell over a racoon that ran under her feet in panic. Gasping, they arrived at the river and waded across. She flopped down with exhaustion on the bank.

"Will it be all right here?" she asked anxiously, staring at Albert in disbelief.

"Who was the criminal who shut you in there?" he asked.

"It was a prank that went wrong. I'll tell you about it later, okay?"

Looking around, Albert said, "I reckon we'd better move if you can manage it. The further from the fire we get the better."

"I'll manage, my eyes are sore though." She rubbed them, leaving her face streaked with soot.

"There's a railway track over there, we'll cross to the other side."

"Won't we be run over by a train?" she asked.

"No, there's only one train a week, on Mondays."

A big harvest-moon floated in the sky and bathed the countryside in a soft light.

"Dominion City is over there, but I won't take you that way." He took her hand again. "How do you feel, can you walk for half an hour?"

"Yes, I'll be okay." She felt happy just walking beside him. "Where are we going?"

"To the Red River, I've a canoe there. I came down the river to see how bad the fire was."

"I can't say how glad I am you came along. It was horrible to be locked in and I was ill part of the time. I've never been so frightened."

"Oh man! How long were you in there?"

"Two days I think. What day was it when I saw you in St. Pierré?"

"Monday, now it's Wednesday." Albert was puzzled. "Did you have anything to eat?"

"No, I wasn't hungry, but I was asleep most of the time."

They slowed down to a steady pace.

"Your holiday didn't get off to a very good start then?"

"No, total disaster. It started when my car broke down and from then on it got worse."

Briefly she told him what had happened. "I still can't believe it happened," she said incredulously.

"I guess not."

"Here I am walking safely in the Manitoba night, thanks to you."

They were standing on the riverbank, looking down at a little, brightly painted birch-bark canoe in the water.

"That's your canoe?" Kathy asked.

21

"It sure is. Have you been in one before?"

"I went canoeing last summer."

"Okay then." They jumped down the bank onto a little strip of sand at the water's edge. Albert reached down into the canoe and took out a life-jacket. "Put that on," he said handing it to her. "Water safety requirements."

The waves lapped softly on the bank as they stepped into the canoe. A startled bird rose off the river and flew into the night. Albert dipped the paddles into the water, drew away from the riverbank and paddled up stream.

Kathy brushed a moth from her face and looked at Albert, remembering the first time she'd seen him. Glow-worms, their little blue lights flickering, danced in circles around them. She sat quietly listening to all the sounds in the bush and wondering about her new-found friendship with Albert, as she watched the ripples of water from the paddles glistening in the moonlight.

"I figured it would be best for me to take you to Emerson. There's a nice motel there where you could get fixed up," he said, viewing her with some concern. "I'll call for you in the morning and take you to the garage for your car. I have to go to St. Pierré anyway."

"Thanks for all you've done for me Albert. That may sound a bit trite, considering you saved my life."

"My pleasure. I'm glad I found you in time."

"What's that strange bird call?" she asked.

"That's the call of the whip-poor-will, a night bird. It's got a big wide beak for eating moths. The moon-moth's wing span is about six inches."

"It's calling 'whip-poor-will', I can hear it, that's lovely," she said listening attentively.

A cool breeze blew in her face and she gradually forgot the horrors of the last few days.

"Brainless idiot, that Jake," Albert said, seeming to pick up on Kathy's thoughts.

"I would have to meet someone like that. He's got a bigoted attitude towards Indians too."

"I guess I'm used to that. People with hang-ups have all sorts of trumped-up reasons for what they think. I reckon I'm immune by now. Hollywood hasn't helped either. We're either portrayed as noble savages or fat slobs."

Kathy paused, then she said, "Those people on the little farms seem to have a pretty tough time. Perhaps it all got to Jake. I was listening to a country western radio station from St. Paul, Minnesota, when I was in the car. Bob Dylan's song 'A Hard Rain's A Gonna Fall', one of his protest songs. That seems a better way of handling hard times or bad situations, don't you think?"

"That's for sure. He comes from the same sort of background as Jake. Do you hear that coyote out there?"

"Is that what it is? It's a lonely sound." She sat listening to the lapping of the water on the stones, the chirping of crickets and the honking of water-fowl as they rose out of the water at their approach. Her heart was full of thankfulness that she was alive. To think I nearly lost it all, she thought.

"That coyote out there," Kathy said, "it reminds me, I saw a timber-wolf this morning while I was shut in the stable. I woke with hail rattling on the roof and a big clap of thunder. When I looked out there was a large timber-wolf in the yard, standing by an old tractor and staring in my direction."

"They're not often so far over this way. There are about eighty of them out there, but most towards Ontario. Canada has the biggest concentration of wolves apart from Russia, I think."

"There was something so dramatic about it," she said, "the wolf and the storm. It looked as if it was lit by a spotlight."

"They're a brainy lot wolves, and more feared than they should be."

"The Romans had a she-wolf on a fourth century coin, because of the legend of Romulus and Reemus being nursed by a she-wolf."

"I remember that now you speak of it." He paused, then asked tentatively, "When are you going home Kathy?"

"I've another ten days, leaving on the Saturday. Do you live on a reserve Albert?"

"No, thankfully. They're dire places to live in. I did a university course, something like the one you're on. I'm also working on Indian and Aboriginal Rights."

"How's that all going?"

"I guess we're making some progress. One point; we like to be called Native Americans rather than Indians."

"Well that is correct, no one can argue with that. I hope you don't mind me asking, are you married Albert?"

He was silent for a few minutes, then he said, "No, I'm not," before adding, "you're not treading on anyone's toes, if that makes any difference. How about you? Am I going to make anyone jealous?"

"No," she said quietly. "I've found the dating game a bit of a minefield."

"That's how I'd put it too."

"Those lights up there, is that Emerson?"

"That's it, we'll be there in a few minutes."

"The first thing I'll do when I get to the motel will be to jump in a hot bath."

Albert stopped paddling. "This is where we get out. Here give me your hand, I don't want to have to fish you out of the water next. I'll take you over to the motel, they'll be okay. There'll be a few other smoky people there tonight, so you'll fit in."

"I can't thank you enough and I'll always remember this night," Kathy said on arriving at the motel.

"I hope you're feeling better in the morning. I'll come for you about eleven," he said. "How would that do?"

"Just great. I hope you'll be okay too." She took his rough hand in hers.

He waved and was gone.

CHAPTER 6

Kathy woke next morning and lay in bed thinking of the last few days. She thought about Albert. I wonder how he feels about me? Probably not much at all.

She decided that the one thing she must do was buy a straw hat. Beside that, a new shirt and shorts, what she had, reeked of smoke.

As she left the motel she noticed a man in the lounge whom she thought she'd seen before. He didn't recognize her, so she thought no more of it.

After buying her new clothes Kathy wandered round the town. The border check-point between America and Canada was busy with travellers. Some wooden houses by the river were built on raised platforms to protect them from water when the river rose, a reminder of flood potential. She was impressed by the many tall trees along the Red River. While waiting for Albert, she sat down to eat an ice-cream in the shade. Will it be the last time I see him? she wondered. To thank him for helping her, she'd bought him a present, a little book of Canadian poems.

She was finishing her ice-cream, when a car drove up not far away and the man she's seen in the motel a little earlier got out, carrying a small wooden case.

Returning to the motel she changed her clothes to be ready for Albert. There was no one in the lounge when he came in later. Kathy got up to greet him, thinking he was ready to leave. Instead he asked, "Do you think we might have a cup of coffee before we go?"

"Yes I'll order some. Is the fire out in the bush?"

"Yes for sure, with the help of about twenty fire-fighters. You look a bit better this morning though your eyes still look a bit sore."

"Are you all right? Your eyes sore? That smoke can really make them sting," Kathy said.

"Sure, I'm all right."

"I had to buy new clothes, what I had on were a mess and all smoky."

"That Jake has a lot to answer for I reckon. What does he think he's playing at?"

Kathy held out her gift. "For you, to say thanks for all you've done for me."

"That's very kind of you. Thanks." He looked at it with pleasure and slipped it into his pocket. "Glad I was on hand at the time. Little did I know when I first saw you in St. Pierré what I was letting myself in for."

"Don't go mocking me," she said, laughing.

"Seriously though," he continued, "it's a rather dangerous place for a girl on her own. There's all sorts of animals out there. Most people who live round here have guns. Keep near the road and don't wander about in the bush, there's swamps around here too and you can literally get lost. I know it's all very alluring, but it's dangerous, if you don't know what you are doing."

"Like you," she said quickly. "Very alluring and dangerous. I couldn't have put it better myself."

Jokingly too, he said, "I might even bite, if you corner me that is."

"Then I'd have teeth marks for the rest of my life and could show all my friends what a real Indian did to me."

"Very savage tribe the Crees."

"You belong to the Cree tribe?"

"I sure do. They were the eastern forest hunters and fishers, the southern most subartic tribe. From Manitoba they spread across into Saskatchewan."

"I want to find out all sorts of things. Manitoba, that word's poetic."

"Do you know how the province got its name?"

"No."

"It's named after the Great Spirit Manitou," Albert explained. "A narrow channel of water connecting the north and south basins of Lake Manitoba, laps and pounds ashore like the drums of the Indian Manitou. You know what Kathy, we've got to go," he said, rising.

"Right then."

"Here's my phone number in case you need some help," he told her, handing her a piece of paper torn from a notebook.

"Thanks very much, I hope it doesn't come to that," she said laughingly. As they drove off, Kathy said, "My dad came from Canada, Saskatchewan, near Fort Carlton."

"So you're half Canadian then?"

"Well, a bit. I wanted so much to come here, to see Canada for myself. I'm also hoping to trace a great-aunt of mine who lived round here at one time. I've been so looking forward to coming here."

"Things are not always what you figure they'll be."

"I'm not disappointed, in spite of the fire, but I know I haven't seen much of it yet."

"I reckon that's okay then."

"Can we stop before we get to the garage? I'd like a photo of you if you don't mind."

"Sure, I'd like one too." He slowed down, stopping on the grit road.

"I want one to remind me of you when I'm home again," she said, unable to disguise a note of sadness in her voice as she put the camera back in the car.

Albert walked across to the other side of the road. Beside the dried up ditch of tangled bulrushes and grass he stood a minute or two, looking somewhere in the far distance towards a thin blue line of trees. Kathy followed. The heat was rising from the grit road and the only sound was that of grasshoppers and other insects chirping and humming in the grass.

Then Albert turned and said, "Kathy, there's a country western night at a casino in Winnipeg on Friday, Bob Dylan'll be there, would you like to go with me?"

"Oh yes, I'd love to go."

He put out his hand and brushed her cheek with his fingers. "Where will you be staying?"

"I'll be at the St Pierré motel."

"Okay, let's get your car."

CHAPTER 7

Kathy was getting used to the dusty grit roads and knew as she drove to the village of Vita, to shut the windows quickly when someone in a car or truck came towards her. She now had her straw hat like other people. There's something about Manitoba, she thought, I've never felt so relaxed anywhere before.

She drove over the single-lined railway track that crossed the road into the village, consisting of a church, motel, modern looking senior school and two stores. There were several streets of small white painted wooden houses, behind white picket fences, enclosing gardens of bright flowers.

Stopping at one store to buy an ice-cream, she sat down on the steps in a shady patch away by herself. She wanted to think. So much had happened to her over the last few days, how would the rest of her holiday turn out, she wondered. It had all seemed so simple when she left Winnipeg, but there had been Jake and his family, the bushfire and now there was Albert. It made her sad to think of going home and leaving him behind, perhaps never to see him again. I'll be lonely for the rest of the life she thought. All I'll have of him will be a photograph.

Kathy felt a cold wet nose pushed under her arm and looking down, saw a black and white collie dog. She patted the furry head in her lap and felt her sadness drift away. The kindly dog sensed my sadness and wanted to cheer me up, she mused.

"You're a lovely dog," she said gently in its ear. "Thank you for making me feel better." She looked across to the old man who owned the dog and waved to him.

"Here Sally," he called and the dog obeyed.

Now I'll look around the store, Kathy decided. She found it fascinating. There were all sorts of things piled up on tables. To her, it looked like a giant jumble sale. Socks were mixed up with apples, topped by straw hats. Writing paper slid among the slippers in glorious chaos. Packets of sunflower seeds, a staple diet in the area, were stacked up next to the jam. Boxes of bright plastic trinkets, purses and small pictures shared space with boxes of cucumbers, corn, plums and honey-melon. Leaning on the counter, sacks of breakfast cereals lined up with sacks of flour. Staked on some underwear, the bread was too near the washing soap.

Kathy helped herself to a bottle of Root Beer and took it over to the counter where the store-keeper was weighing the jowls of a pig, complete with ear. Deciding there was nothing more she wanted, she made her way to the door, past a sliding stack of doormats.

She had to wait at the bottom of the steps for an old man to wheel a giant orange pumpkin along in a wheelbarrow.

In spite of the heat, Kathy decided to pay a short visit to Steinbach. What she saw on reaching the town was not what she expected. It looked like a busy frontier town. Every kind of car, truck, bulldozer, combine-harvester and farm implement imaginable, filled every available spot. It was, Kathy thought, choc-a-block with people buying and selling or browsing around, everyone looking for a bargain.

In contrast to this, Kathy was amazed to see one side of the street lined with huge wooden crates, heaped up with gigantic bright green water melons. She watched intrigued as people squeezed melons into the back seats of cars and trucks.

One trader didn't like her taking photographs of his stall, which made her all the more interested in his transactions. She got the impression he was fiddling something, making sure he kept his back to her if he could. Maybe I'm imagining things, she thought; hot day, strange country and so much more to see. I've had enough for one day, she decided, I'm going back to St. Pierré. Tomorrow is a special day, I'm going out with Albert Thunder.

When Kathy phoned her mother and father in the evening she told them about the marvellous time she was having, but she didn't tell them about Albert. How could she say, Mum, I met this Indian called Albert Thunder? Or I was locked in an old stable, there was a bushfire and an Indian let me out and saved my life? Even Dad, who was borne in Canada, wouldn't know what to think if I told him that, even though things have changed for the Native Americans since he was here. Anyway, she thought, there's no knowing how Albert and I will make out. There's something very special about our relationship. I don't feel shy with him. He doesn't seem to have any hang-ups. She pondered these and other questions about him when alone and couldn't wait till she saw him again.

As she studied the map of Manitoba in the evening, trying to decide where to go the next day, she felt a great affinity with the place. I think it's cast a spell on me, she mused as she lay in bed. She fell asleep remembering a song she'd heard on the radio, 'Moody Manitoba'.

CHAPTER 8

At the St Pierré motel, Kathy had found a friend in Jacqui, the proprietress, she having spent a holiday in England the year before.

"I could give you something to soothe your eyes," she'd said when Kathy had arrived and told her she wished to stay at the motel for the rest of her holiday.

"Where are you going today?" she asked, when she saw Kathy ready to go out.

"I thought I'd just look around St. Pierré and take it easy," she replied, "I'm going out on a date tonight."

About lunchtime Kathy went into the little café where, for the first time she'd seen Albert and she pondered on how things had changed in such a short time.

A party of young people sat at the other tables. She gathered by their speech that they were from England, but she didn't want to get into conversation with them. They'll just think I'm a local girl, she hoped.

Kathy sat thinking about her grandmother's sister and wondered where she'd ended up. I hope I can find out something about her, she said to herself. She wouldn't have been living in St. Pierré, I know because it was a French-Canadian pioneering settlement; hardly any English people, even now.

After a little stroll around the town, she went back early to the motel, excited about going out in the evening. It would be something quite different from anything else she'd ever been to. More than anything, she said to herself, I'll just love being with Albert. She longed to know him better, but felt the outcome was impossible to predict.

CHAPTER 9

When Albert called for Kathy she was much impressed by his appearance, his natural poise and gentleness of manner. He was dressed in a cowboy outfit, jeans, shirt, apache tie, cowboy boots and hat.

His eyes lit up when he saw her. "You look very beautiful," he commented.

She smiled at him. "Thanks, you look drop dead gorgeous."

"I don't reckon I know what to say to that, but I've brought a cowboy hat for you. I thought you might like it."

She put it on. "I feel a bit of a fraud. I haven't even been on a horse."

When they reached the casino where the event was being held, Kathy thought it looked like the set of a Hollywood Western, so many people wore jeans, fringed jackets, cowboy hats and boots. There were some Canadian Mounties with guns in their holsters moving among the crowd in the car park.

"Looking for people carrying drugs," Albert remarked. "They'll know who they're looking for I reckon."

Outside, the tantalizing smell of popcorn filled the air and the vendor had a job to keep up with all his customers. Albert bought popcorn for both of them. "Here," he said, handing her a bag, "see how you like that."

Country music filled the air outside and inside the hall. Decorated with hunting trophies, moose and deer antlers, buffalo horns and all manner of other artefacts, it looked impressive. There were framed, antique licences for hunting and pictures of pioneering days. Kathy bought a facsimile of a licence to kill and hunt buffalo in Manitoba during the hunting season. "That's a momento for me to take home," she told Albert.

There were seats and tables round the hall and in the centre.

"I guess we'd better sit by the wall," Albert suggested. "If we sit in the centre we'll have people bumping into us all evening."

Kathy seated herself and ate her popcorn while watching all that went on. Albert went off for drinks. He came back with Root Beer and Canada Dry. "That okay?" he asked. "I'm driving, I'll have to stick with soft drinks."

"That's fine, all I want, thanks."

At one point, two Indians spotted Albert and came over to speak to him. "Hi there you guys," one said, taking a close look at Kathy.

"This is Kathy Roberts, a zoology student from England," Albert said proudly.

"I'm here exploring the Southeast. I've only been here a few days."

"Albert's a fast worker. Great guy," one said, grinning at Albert. Kathy blushed. "Yes I know."

"You're sure okay there," drawled the other. "Have a good time. See you Albert. We've got to catch up with our partners over there."

They went on their way saying they were pleased to meet Kathy. She took it as a genuine remark.

"They're from the Roseau Reserve," Albert explained. "It's a little north of Emerson. We went that way the night of the fire."

"I'll never forget that night," she said, putting her hand into his. "Was I glad to see you?"

"I know, you were sure in a fine state. I couldn't think how you got there."

The Native American singer, Buffy St. Marie mounted the platform to a burst of applause and started the proceedings with a song that she herself wrote, 'Piney Wood Hills'. "I'm a rambler and a rover," she sang. Kathy liked the singer and the song feeling it a pleasant start to the show. Johnny Cash got everyone charmed by his lovely voice, he got a great reception. Kathy loved Bob Dylan's songs, sung in his own inimitable style. His repertoire of hits included, 'A Hard Rain's A Gonna Fall', 'The Times They Are A-Changing' and to finish, 'Blowing in the Wind', all received with rapturous applause.

"He must be a very sensitive person," Albert said.

"Yes, he must be. Thanks for a lovely evening."

Albert and Kathy stood outside after the show enjoying the cool air. "I've really enjoyed myself," she said.

"I'm glad, you deserve some fun on your holiday. Thanks for your company. We'll have to do something else before you go home. When do you finish university Kathy?"

"Next summer. I'm studying at Cardiff University, Wales. Do you know where that is?"

"I reckon I do. It's not far from Bristol, near Peter Scott's Wildfowl Reserve at Slimridge. I've been corresponding with a guy at Bristol Zoo."

"Is that so? I haven't been to Slimridge yet. I'll have to go when I get back home."

"That's where Canada-Geese spend winter isn't it? I've seen a film about it. If ever you spend time in Canada in the 'fall' you'll have the poignant experience of seeing the long skeins of geese leaving and flying south. Every fall the honking of wildfowl on their way south, day after day, night after night. When it's dark you can't see them, but you hear the whir of their wings and their calling to one another. Finally they're all gone and winter settles in. Then there's just silence. Most of the other birds leave too and there's a kind of silent emptiness. Then it starts to snow and blow until the end of March."

"I could imagine the winter when you describe it like that, strange to think the birds have been doing that for thousands of years."

"I guess we'd better be on our way too," Albert said.

At St. Pierré it was quiet after the noise of the town. Along the line of the horizon little blips of lightning flashed. "I see that most nights," Kathy said, "but the storms don't always come up this far."

"They change with the seasons."

They both lapsed into silence, the silence of two people who empathize with each other. Kathy played with her cowboy hat. Then Albert said, "Would you like us to go out somewhere on Sunday?"

"Yes I'd love to. Where were you thinking of going?"

"Lake Bronson, Minnesota, how about that?"

"That would be just great."

"Right, I'll pick you up here about eleven, okay?"

He put his arm round her. She held on to him, not wanting him to go and lifted her face to him for their first kiss.

"See you Sunday," he said, releasing her.

"Here's your hat, thanks for the loan of it Albert." She waved as he drove away, knowing she'd see him soon. A coyote howled and not far away another answered as she closed the door.

34

CHAPTER 10

Kathy found her way to the Roseau River the following day. She sat on a high bank and looked down on the river's meandering course. It's a well-worn path, she said to herself, someone must use it regularly.

In the clearing of the bush nearby, a small house sat peeping through the trees and she could hear the clatter of a pail in an outhouse as someone moved about.

Then she became fascinated by a large anthill a little distance from her, that she hadn't noticed when sitting down. It was about four feet high, and the scene of great activity, which seemed to be all to no purpose. However she knew enough about ants to tell what all the frantic effort was about. The ants had worn a deep narrow track through the grass and were using it like a super-highway. She was contemplating the scene all around when she became aware of the soft clip, clop of hooves and from a track to her right a few yards ahead an Indian man emerged. He led a horse on which a woman rode carrying a small child wrapped in a shawl. Another Indian with a staff followed. Kathy wondered why the child was wrapped in a shawl on such a hot day. They were dressed in Indian clothes and cross the path without looking to left or right, entering the bush on the opposite side where the track continued. Kathy sat silently gazing at the spot where she'd seen them disappear, as slowly the muffled sound of horses' hooves died away.

Wondering about them after they'd gone, Kathy sat enjoying the peace of the place, the smell of wood, ferns and moss. She was admiring some giant size, bright red and white spotted toadstools the size of a teaplate, when an old woman carrying a pail, came towards her from the direction of the house. She went down the steep little track to the river's edge and filled her pail.

On returning she looked over to Kathy and with a German accent said, "Hi, are you fine?"

"Yes thanks."

She put her pail down by Kathy, "Would you like to come and have a drink?"

"Yes I'd like to."

"Okay then, you come wid me."

Kathy rose and picked up the pail of water. "I'll carry it for you," she said, "I'm Kathy."

"I'm Agnes, come along."

Her house was cool, sparsely furnished, but painted with bright colours. "You sit and I'll get a glass. Thanks for carrying the pail."

A girl of about fifteen sat in a chair at the table. "This is Joana, my grand-daughter. She come wid crab-apples for me."

The girl smiled, but said nothing and carried on shelling peas. She had a pile of corn-on-the-cob stacked beside her on the table.

"Have you lived here long?" Kathy asked Agnes.

"Most of my life. I came to this part of the country when I married fifty years ago. My mother came with her parents to this part of the country when my mother was a child. Vot do you do?"

"I'm on holiday," Kathy said, sipping the soft cold water from the glass Agnes had placed for her on the table.

"Take a cookie," Agnes urged, putting down a plate of currant biscuits. "Vot do you do when you're not on holiday?"

"I'm a student from England."

"Oh dat is nice. My grand-daughter is in grade eleven at school, she finishes next year. She is all busy with work." Agnes sat down and picked up some knitting. "I knit slippers for my grandchildren, for Christmas, nine pairs and some mittens."

Kathy told her about the Indians she had seen. "Where do they live?" she asked.

"They're not here anymore, you must have seen the ghosts. Some people, they see them. Once I saw them. How you fill now?"

She obviously didn't want to talk about them, so Kathy said, "What do you grow in your garden?"

"Lots corn, bins, peas, cucumbers, lettuce, tomatoes, carrots, dill, honey-melons, all sorts of tings. There's lots of fruit in the bush too. I bottle lots crab-apples and do cucumber pickles with dill and all."

"That's some garden. You're always busy then?"

"I kip busy. On Sunday I had my family here for the day. We had soup for dinner, made ham and cabbage rolls, boiled potatoes, made salad and jello. For tea we had dough-rings, buns, cookies and sandwiches. The children played outside. You all had a good time, didn't you Joana?"

"That's for sure Gran."

"Do you see any bears round here?" Kathy asked.

Joana replied, "Sometimes we do. The children at school, the ones who live off the highway, like here, are told to carry a tin of dried peas in their lunch-box. Then if they see a bear after getting off the school bus, they have to rattle the tin of peas to make the bear run away."

"Oh goodness," Kathy said, somewhat amazed. "I'll have to start carrying a tin of dried peas too."

"The little kids got a holiday one day last term," Joana said, "because a skunk got into the ventilating system. It was a terrible smell."

"I should think so too," Kathy said. "Do you like school?"

"It's okay now. I didn't like it when I was small. One teacher made a girl go outside when she was naughty and kneel on the gravel path for an hour, with her hands on her head. It was a hot day as well. Her mum and dad were right mad about it. The teacher had to stop doing it."

"I should think so too."

Kathy got up to go. Agnes said, "We'll walk up the road with you."

"Thank you both very much for a lovely time. I'll remember you when I get home."

Kathy was on her way back to St. Pierré before she remembered about Aunt Ida. I was so taken with those people that I forgot to ask them about her, she thought.

CHAPTER 11

"I'm going to Lake Bronson with a friend Jacqui," Kathy called, as she was on her way out of the motel.

"Have a good time," Jacqui said, coming from the kitchen.

The day was bright and sunny, but a bit cooler when Kathy saw Albert coming and ran out to meet him.

"This is so exciting," she said happily. "I'll even get an American stamp on my passport." She had it in her hand. "Would you recognise me?" she asked, showing Albert her photograph.

"Sure it looks like you. Enough for them to let you through anyway."

"Would you show me yours?" she asked eagerly.

Albert handed over his. "I've another name," he said, "but I prefer that one. Most of us at one time had two names. Native Americans believed that if an enemy used their real name, the enemy could destroy their soul. The real name of Pocahontas was Matoaka. Did you know that?"

"No. Is that so? That's interesting." She looked at his photo. He had the distinctive Indian features, high cheek bones and a firm mouth, but it was his eyes she found so irresistible.

"Well, what's the verdict?" he asked.

"Like I said before, just drop dead gorgeous."

"That'll do me," he said whimsically.

They went through the little border-crossing at Tolstoi without much questioning. "Quite a privilege," Kathy commented, "to be more or less waved through into another country."

"The local people cross back and forth all the time, but if you're not back the same day the American State Police'll come looking for you," Albert explained. "This highway, the 59, through from Lake Bronson to Winnipeg, was the old Crow Indian Trail. They travelled up to the Hudson's Bay fur trading post at Fort Garry. Most of the area to the west was swamp, so the trail through Tolstoi was the only safe route at the time. There are Indian stone tepee rings and council rings a mile north of Reston, on a glacial outwash; a prehistoric Indian Campsite. It's by Pipestone Creek, near the Saskatchewan border, part of the Southern Moose Mountain Trail that runs from Fort Ellice, west of Winnipeg to Carlyle. The whole distance to Edmonton Alberta is about six hundred miles."

Kathy listened with great interest. "I wish I could go back in time and see the Indians on the trail. Sometimes when I go down a little path in the bush, I get the impression that Indians have just left and will shortly be back. I saw some yesterday by the Roseau River, but an old woman who lives there told me I'd seen ghosts of Indians who walked there sometimes."

"Indian believe in ghosts. Some say that a person is three things, a body, a spirit and a ghost," Albert said.

"I like that," Kathy replied, "ghosts in the woods instead of in buildings. Looking round, she said, "I believe some people get the creeps in wilderness places."

"That's because they let their imaginations run wild. You can't let yourself do that. You'll scare yourself to death if nothing else. Anyway people who live close to nature don't feel that way. I guess they are too in tune with nature to let it worry them."

Kathy spotted two deer sitting in the grass a few yards off. "Look deer, you can just see the top of their heads and their ears sticking up in the grass."

"Yes, I figure we'll probably see some more."

"Not many people live round here," Kathy remarked. "I can't imagine myself living in such a lonely place." She turned to Albert, "I suppose having family makes a difference. What family have you got Albert?"

"Mother, an elder brother Robert, he's a lawyer. Then I have a sister Mary, she's eighteen, keen on art. My father died three years ago. How about you Kathy? Tell me about your family."

"Mum, Dad, brother Andy, sixteen. My mother and father own and run a small hotel in Devon, the south coast of England. It seems a very long way away."

"I reckon it does, but here's our destination."

"Is this Lake Bronson?"

"That's for sure."

They'd arrived at a picnic area, rather crowded with families all enjoying the water.

"It's lovely here," Kathy said, looking around at the wide lake in a clearing of trees. "I'd like to have a swim."

"If you want to go in it's okay if you stay where the other people are, where the lifeguard is. It goes down deep like a shelf in the middle. There's weeds in there too, over by that island, so you'll have to keep away from them, they'll twist round your legs."

"Aren't you going in then?"

"No, I don't want to risk the car being stolen and losing our passports, cameras and everything. That can happen down here."

"Okay then, I've got my dress over my swimsuit, I can jump in," she said throwing her dress into the back of the car. She didn't stay long in the water, but came back and wrapped herself in a towel before sitting down. "Oh that was cold, but I enjoyed it. Let's have something to eat shall we?"

They sat talking and eating their sandwiches, then Albert reached over behind Kathy and picked up a couple of bluejay feathers. He stuck them in his hair and announced, "Me Big Chief Thunder."

Kathy laughing looked around and found another feather. Putting it in her hair, she said, "Me Lightning." Looking at Albert she couldn't keep a straight face. "That could cause quite a storm," she said and lay back laughing.

"I reckon it'd be more like a thunder-bolt," he replied. "Can I comb your hair?" He held it in his hand. "It's lovely and silky."

She handed him the comb.

"How's that?" he asked when he'd finished.

"Fine," she said stroking his face. "I can't comb yours. You've got it set like a fan at the back and tied so nicely, I'd just make a mess of it. Isn't it strange, we come from very difference cultures; yet we're drawn together like this."

Taking her hand he said, "We were all hunters and gatherers once, now we all go to the supermarket."

"Now we are some of us wildlife experts and conservationists."

"Once the law round here was, if you don't hunt you don't eat," he said solemnly.

"I expect it was. In Britain at one time, the king and his courtiers went hunting in the royal forests for stag and wild boar. People can walk now in Windsor Great Park and the New Forest; that isn't new, it's a thousand years old," she said. "Native Americans have their myths and legends, very like the myths and legends of ancient Greece. We have too. Have you heard of King Arthur and the Round Table and Queen Bodica?"

"Sure I have. Like the Greek and Roman deities, in our legends the people were of elemental descent. They had supernatural powers, could throw huge rocks for miles and shake mountains. Spirits lived in lakes and forests. People believed in magic because that was the only way that some things could be explained, metamorphosis for instance."

"How have people got facts so wrong. Native Americans were always the baddies in the old films children used to watch in cinemas on Saturday morning before television. It's taking a long time for attitudes to change isn't it?"

"During the Second World War, members of the Navajo Tribe who served in the American Marines, transmitted and received radio messages because their language couldn't be translated by linguistic experts in either Japanese or German armies. Over three thousand Navajos served in the armed forces. Several Native Americans won the Congressional Medal of Honour, but somehow the Navajos missed out, though they served at the front line."

"It's all a very uphill task I must say. It upsets me. I'm going to change the subject. How did Indians know south from north on days when there was no sun?"

"There are ways. For instance, the grass grows the way of the prevailing wind, see it's bent towards the east. It doesn't need a brain surgeon to work out from that, where the north is."

"I've heard about the Chinook wind that blows from the west in the spring. It's supposed to give people the wanderlust."

"Primitive instinct, itchy feet," Albert replied, tickling Kathy's feet with a feather, when she wasn't looking, which sent her rolling about laughing again. "We'd better be going I guess."

"Let's then, I'll get dressed." When she came back she asked, "Could we walk through a bit of the bush on our way home? We might see some animals or just enjoy the walk."

"No, is the short answer to that."

"Yes." She sat down.

"No."

Kathy turned towards him. "Why not?" she demanded.

He took her hand and pulled her up. "Because I've got alarm bells ringing in my head, that's why." He turned to face her and looking into her eyes he said, "You are a tempting little miss and I don't want us to get up to something we afterwards wished we hadn't go up to, if you get my drift. I've got a conscience even if it's

41

an Indian one. I'm an all or nothing man and it's rather unusual circumstances you've got to admit. Okay?"

She momentarily hung her head, "We won't go for a walk in the bush then. I forgot to set my alarm clock, I guess I don't know myself very well."

"I guess I don't either," Albert said gently.

"I guess not," she replied, "but I'm not the only one that's tempting around here," she laughed, stroking his hair. "I think," she said, "you're too compassionate to be passionate Albert."

He put his arm around her, "You could be very wrong about that madam."

"That's good," she said, resting her head on his shoulder.

"Come on, let's go shall we? We could go a different way home," he suggested.

"I'd like that."

Just before they reached the Canadian border, they came to the tiny village of Orleans just as a freight-train about a quarter of a mile long, whistled its lonely call and rumbled southward. A one-eyed dog, sitting on the steps of the post office was the only sign of life in the place.

"I forgot to tell you," Kathy said, when I went to Jake's home they said there'd been a moose in their field the day before and their neighbours had phoned the conservation officer."

"I heard about that, but I'm afraid by the time he'd caught up with the moose it was cut up into small pieces and packed in the deep-freeze of a farmer across at Sandown."

"Really?"

"Sure, but he'll get taken to court and fined about a thousand dollars, but that won't bring back the moose."

Jacqui was at the motel door when they got back. "Have you had a good day?" she asked.

"Yes lovely thanks. Jacqui this is Albert, my rescuer who saved me from the bush-fire."

"I figured you might be," Jacque said, shaking Albert's hand. "Have you got time to come in?"

"Okay, I'll come in if you want me to Kathy."

"Course, come on in. Thanks Jacqui."

While they were sitting talking about their lives and their time together and drinking the coffee provided by Jacqui, Albert said,

"John phoned me yesterday to ask if I would like to go to an auction sale of buffalo coats. The Winnipeg Police Department are selling off the coats. I'd like to go and buy one. Would you like to go with me?"

"Yes I would. I might even buy one. Did the Mounties really wear buffalo coats at one time?"

"Sure, still do, on occasions. Over in Edmonton, Alberta they can't get enough of them. John figures they'll sell for around thirty-five dollars each. Some need major repairs though, so we have to watch we get good ones."

"I wonder if a buffalo coat will go down well in Torquay? What does John do at the police department?"

"He works on fingerprints."

"Is that so?"

"The times they are a-changing," he said. "Not so long ago it looked as if the Native Americans would just become a theatrical display. Now they are getting all the education they can and getting on in a variety of careers, like me."

"I hope many more will take heart and do the same. There's lots of books written about Native Americans now."

"That can only be a good thing, ignorance was much to blame for a lot of bad things that happened," he said. Kathy noticed a steely glint in his eyes, "Let's not get bogged down with all that though," he remarked.

"Have you known John long?"

"Since we were boys at school."

"What sort of things did you two get up to?"

"The usual stuff, went a bit wild sometimes I guess. Local phone calls were free, so we were on the party line a lot. There were five families on each line, so up to thirty people could use the line. Some spoke in German, some Ukrainian to keep the conversation private. Sometimes half a dozen were on at one time. We got tired of one woman always listening in to our conversation, so John and I put a stop to it. It was easy, knowing the background noises, dog barking, someone saying a child's name, to know just who was listening. We decided to pretend we knew a lot of gossip about her and talked about a funny story we said was going round. It was probably not believable, but it stopped her, she got the hint."

"It's nice to have a friend from childhood."

"That's for sure. I'd better be going Kathy."

Outside, they put their arms round one another. "What are you doing tomorrow?" Albert asked.

"I don't know yet. I'll see how I feel, but thanks for a lovely day."

"I enjoyed myself too," he said stooping to give her a kiss. "See you on Wednesday."

I'm lucky, she thought as he drove away, to have found someone so special.

CHAPTER 12

In the morning Kathy made up her mind she couldn't spend another day in the car. The temperature was already soaring up too high for comfort.

Quite on the spur of the moment she decided to take the Greygoose bus that passed the door and spend the day on her own in Winnipeg. That decided, she boarded the bus half an hour later and sat down on a front seat, wanting to relax and enjoy the ride. Then her attention was drawn to a young man with long fair hair, talking to the bus driver. He'd stood waiting at the bus stop with her in St. Pierré. The driver was telling him he would have to get off, as he didn't have quite enough money for his ticket.

He was at the point of turning to leave the bus, when Kathy put down half a dollar for the driver. "Towards the young man's fare," she said.

The young man received his ticket and turned gratefully to her. "Thanks very much for that," he said, as she took her seat again.

He stopped beside her, "You're English?"

"Yes, on holiday."

"Me too. May I sit with you?"

"Sure," she replied reassuringly. "I'm Kathy Roberts."

"I'm Tim Marshall. I've actually had a bit of bad luck. I lent some money to my girlfriend. She was supposed to meet me in St. Pierré this morning with the money. We're staying in Grunthal for a horse-riding holiday. When she didn't turn up to meet me I phoned the house where she's staying and the person answering, told me she'd gone out last night with another girl and two boys from Grunthal. So, I've been stood up and robbed at the same time."

"How will you manage for money today?"

"I'll get some from a bank in Winnipeg. I was really fed up about it and then not to have enough money for the bus! It was good of you to help out. Where are you off to?"

"Winnipeg, nowhere in particular."

"When are you going back home?"

"Saturday afternoon flight," Kathy told him. "This is my fourth week. I spent two weeks in Winnipeg with an aunt and uncle before going down to St. Pierré."

"Had a good time?"

"Yes seen a lot of interesting places."

"Very different from home," Tim commented. "I don't think I'd like to live here though."

"My father was a Canadian and I have family living here, so I don't feel strange. I love it all. I'll miss it so much when I go home."

"Don't you feel lonely, wandering about on your own?"

"No. I hired a car, but it's so hot and dusty driving around on the grit roads. I didn't feel I could stand another day of it."

"Good thinking, and lucky for me. Do you think as we are both at a loose end we could spend the day together? I'm feeling rather fed up."

Kathy agreed. She felt stressful about Albert. Things seemed somehow so unreal. "That would be fine," she replied. "Sometimes holidays can be a bit like that can't they? Too much expectation I suppose. Well if nothing else it makes us glad to be back home."

They were silent for a while, taking in the panorama, then Tim got back to the conversation. "I like all the little post-boxes outside people's houses. Funny, isn't it, we would feel worried to have our post left outside in England and in bad weather have to go down the drive for it."

"I feel somehow, that we are spoiled in Britain. I know there are unfortunate people there too, but most feel glad to be back after being abroad, don't you think? So many people would just love to have a British passport."

"I'm a student," Tim said, "so I've been trying to see as much of the world as I can before I get too many commitments."

"I'm a student too."

"I thought you probably were. What's your subject?"

"Zoology, I finish next year."

"Mine's Engineering, I finish next year too."

"I'm looking forwards to finishing my course," Kathy said, "and getting my degree. It really is a big hurdle to cross isn't it?"

"I know, there were times when I thought I'd never finish. Here we are then, now I'll be able to get some money again, and get something to eat."

"That little diner over there looks all right. Isn't this fun? It's a bit like a blind date," Kathy remarked.

"Yes," Tim laughed, "better because it's unexpected."

"Funny," Kathy said, "life can go chugging along and suddenly out of the blue a surprise comes down." She was really thinking of Albert, but she felt he was not up for discussion. Instead she listened to a country western song, on the radio, 'Sunday Morning Coming Down'. Somehow she felt it depicted the pathos of city life for the poor at the bottom of the pile.

"It really speaks the truth about a life at the bottom of the pile, as it is for some," Tim said. "I've never lived like that, but that song portrays it like it is."

"Just what I was thinking."

They were wandering through a shopping arcade later, enjoying all the new sights and sounds when Kathy said, "I love that smell, someone's burning josh-sticks."

"It's coming from that boutique," Tim said, "the one with the bead curtains on the door."

"I must go in and sniff around, I love that sort of incense smell. Would you mind if I do?"

"No, I'll come too."

Outside again, a speaker spilled out loud music, Chinese bells tinkled in the breeze, blending with the pop song 'Angel of the Morning'. The whole place was a brilliant cascade of colour and sound.

"I didn't expect things to be so way-out in Winnipeg," Kathy said. "This is more so than some of the cities at home, isn't it?"

"Quite a contrast from the sticks."

"A very derogatory word don't you think?"

"Guess so," Tim said. "Just the usual remark that towns people have always made about country people and vice versa. You know, city-slicker and so on."

"Some places down in the Southeast of Manitoba are like a 1950s time warp." Kathy said.

She stopped to watch a popcorn toasting machine, where a snowstorm of rising and falling popcorn held her gaze. The smell of it filled the air as the little white balls whirled round and round.

"I feel dizzy," she said, turning to Tim.

The next thing she knew, she was waking up in a hospital bed.

"Where am I?" she asked.

"In the Victoria General Hospital," a nurse told her. "You collapsed in an arcade about an hour ago. Your friend is here waiting to speak to you."

In the strange state Kathy was in, she thought the nurse meant Albert was there, so when she turned round and saw Tim, she couldn't at first think who he was. After a few minutes it began to dawn on her who he was. "It was kind of you to wait here for me Tim. I'm sorry I've mucked up your day," she said.

"I wasn't doing anything anyway, and at least I've got rid of a cheating girlfriend. Thanks for that. You didn't have a handbag, you just had a purse, so you had no identification. I told the nurse your name was Kathy Roberts and gave her my name too."

"Thank you. Do you know when I can go?"

"The nurse didn't say, she just said you had heatstroke. Anyway someone will be along for you soon. I found a phone number on a slip of paper tucked down in the back pocket of your purse. The nurse missed it when she looked, it was such a little scrap of paper. I called the number and told someone you were here and what had happened."

Kathy wasn't sure what Tim had said because a tea-trolley came rattling in just then. She thought he'd said something about making a phone call, but nothing seemed to be making any sense. Tim said, "The doctor was quite happy about you and told me you'd be given some medication when you leave."

"I'm feeling a lot better already."

"You gave me a fright when you didn't come round and had to be brought here. One minute you were perfectly happy and the next you were on the ground."

"I'm glad you were with me. No one would have known who I was if I'd been alone. Just look, I've got one of these funny white hospital gowns on. I haven't been in hospital before."

Tim looked at her, "You look all right to me, like the angel of the morning, in the song we heard just before you fainted."

Just then Albert walked in. He looked rather uneasy as he sat down on Kathy's bed. "How are you feeling? What's been happening? I came straight away when I got the phone call."

He turned to Tim. Kathy, feeling better said, "This is Tim, he phoned you when he found your phone number in my purse."

"Thank you Tim, I've very glad you did."

Kathy, knowing Albert was puzzled by the situation, felt she had some explaining to do. "I'm so pleased to see you Albert," she said sincerely. "I decided on the spur of the moment this morning to have a day in Winnipeg instead of going out for another drive in the sun."

"Kathy kindly paid some of my bus fare, as the driver was about to put me off the bus. My girlfriend went off with another chap and my money."

"Oh boy" That's too bad."

"You can say that again. I was fed up, then Kathy and I decided to make a day of it."

"Don't blame you." Turning to Kathy he said, "You did that all right. I'll go and see the doctor, perhaps it'll be okay for you to leave."

Tim turned to Kathy when they were alone. "I'm sorry, I didn't know you had a boyfriend."

"It's okay, nothing's settled."

"I feel I should go."

"If you want to, I enjoyed your company. Thanks for being such a big help. I really appreciate that. I hope you get a nice girl soon."

"Bye then, look after yourself. I might see you around. Have a great time for the rest of your holiday."

Albert looked around on his return. "Tim's gone then?"

"Probably felt he was in the way. He could see we were more than just good friends."

Albert sat down on the bed. "Guess so, seemed a nice guy."

"Yes he was. We sort of palled up, both being English, far from home, you know. Can't compare with my drop dead gorgeous Native American though."

"Oh is that so? I'm sure pleased to know that." He gave her a kiss. "I was just a bit worried for a minute there."

"What did the doctor say?"

"Said you could go. The medication is waiting at the desk. He said you probably had mild food poisoning and heatstroke. I told him you were sick last week and thought it was through your eating a poisonous mushroom. That and the fire. Are you going to dress?"

"Okay."

"I'll wait for you down at the desk."

"Thanks Albert."

She was glad to get into the car and on her way to St. Pierré.

In bed that night she thought, there can't possibly be anything else that can go wrong. Albert's so sweet, I'm so lucky to have met him.

CHAPTER 13

Kathy woke in the morning feeling her old self and ready to plan another day. When Albert phoned to ask how she felt he was glad to hear her say she was fine.

"Have you figured out what you're doing today?" he asked.

"No, not yet."

"I wondered if you'd be in the Dominion City area at all? I could meet you there about two o'clock if you like."

"All right, I'll do that. I wanted to go there sometime to see if anyone there had known my aunt Ida. I've still found no trace of her."

"Okay then, I'll see you about two, by the courthouse."

"I don't have to bail you out or anything like that?"

"No, that's not on the score."

"Right see you there."

"Bye, take care."

"Bye," she said, putting down the phone. There's one thing about Albert she thought, he's full of surprises.

Dominion City proved to be a busy little market town like the others in the area. She was beginning to feel there was an old world charm about them. In a store she watched a woman take a man's large dark suit off a rail. After admiring it and considering it, she bought it. Obviously her man would find it quite acceptable, if the pleased look on the woman's face was anything to go by. Kathy thought, how sweet and loving, taking home a suit without the need to try it on. It was obviously a present.

After her lunch Kathy walked over to the courthouse and sat in the shade to wait for Albert. Everything was so different from home, the traffic, the buildings and the people. The stores sold things made locally and she wished she could take more of it home with her.

The day was hot and sunny, but she was getting used to the heat. After waiting for a few minutes she noticed an Indian in a formal suit, come out of the courthouse and look around. He came towards her and stood in front of her. She waited for him to speak. He seemed familiar, but she couldn't think who he was. Then to her surprise he asked, "Are you Kathy Roberts?"

51

"Yes, that's me." She got up feeling puzzled. He held out his hand. "You don't know me," he said, "I'm pleased to meet you. I'm Albert's brother Robert. He sent me to look for you, he's been held up. I have to be in the courthouse this afternoon, so Albert suggested that you wait inside for him."

He scrutinized her closely while he spoke. Kathy thought afterwards, it was as if he went into her head, had a good look round and came out again. It didn't bother her however because she had apparently passed the test. "Albert's been telling me about you," he said, hoping to make her feel at ease.

Now he looks like Albert, she thought. "Yes I'll come and wait in the courthouse. Albert and I had rather a weird start to our friendship," she said as she walked with him.

"So I gather. These things happen." He looked closely at her again. "He's a lucky guy," he said, showing her to a seat at the back of the small court. "Albert shouldn't be too long."

What next? she thought, gazing at the rows of heads before her. They were quite an assortment of people, all waiting for proceedings to begin, while court officials bustled about.

A middle-aged woman beside her, brushed a tear from her face.

"Are you all right?" Kathy asked anxiously.

"I'll be fine in a minute I reckon. I've come instead of my father, he's an old man. His cows got into the neighbour's field and ate the grass. The neighbour says my father drove his cows in, as his own grass was all dried up. I hope my father's not prosecuted, it'll make him ill."

"It sounds a very flimsy sort of accusation to me," Kathy said, "I shouldn't worry."

The first case was that of a man who had been caught driving without a licence. He defiantly made a plea that his licence was in the post, so he was bailed to appear at a later date.

Then the case of a man who'd accidentally set fire to a neighbour's hay field while burning his own old grass. It was quickly dealt with.

Kathy patted the arm of the woman next to her who was looking very unhappy about her case coming up. "It won't take long now, you'll soon be out. We all make mistakes," she added reassuringly.

Then Kathy was struck by the sound of clinking chains, and four very unhappy Indians, all chained together, were led in. She was shocked. She felt she's suddenly been transported back in time. This can't be the twentieth century? she thought, wanting to get up and shout or protest about the whole thing.

Just then Albert slipped in beside her on the seat. "Okay?" he asked, "Robert found you then?"

"Yes I'm okay thanks. What's happening to those Indians?"

"Got drunk I guess." Albert said in a whisper. "I'm sorry I was held up. Shall we go out?"

"Right."

Outside, she said angrily, "I found that Indian business so upsetting, horrible, those men all chained up!"

"That's common practise when prisoners are escorted to and from gaol. The guards don't want them running off. They'll just be charged with being drunk and disorderly, fined, and let out again."

"When your brother found me, I couldn't think what he wanted me for. I didn't think of him being your brother, though he does look like you; but not so drop dead gorgeous."

"You're sure hopeless you are Kathy, but thanks."

"Your brother looked me over and said you were a lucky guy, but I won't let it go to my head."

"I know I'm lucky. As for praise going to your head, I don't think you're the dizzy sort."

"Well if I get dizzy I'll just put my head between my knees and take some deep breaths."

"Shall we finish this conversation over coffee?"

"Where?"

"That café over there?"

"Right."

"Sorry I can only stay an hour, I've got some work to do Kathy."

"Much?"

"Sure have."

They were sitting talking about their families, when Kathy said, "I feel as if I've been away from home for months, instead of just three weeks. I'll miss you for the rest of my life if I don't see you again," she added, putting her hand on his.

"Things have a way of working out I reckon." He spoke candidly, tightening his grip on her hand.

"You mean some things are meant to be?"

"I guess so. Perhaps it depends on how badly you want something."

"I didn't find out anything about my Aunt Ida today."

"No?"

"I'll keep trying. I forgot to tell you about the day I went to Steinbach and the melon man, that was after I left you on Wednesday."

"What was that then?"

"I was looking at the giant water-melons in big wooden crates, when I stopped at a stall to take a photograph. When the trader saw me he was angry and told me to clear off. I think he was up to a fiddle."

"Queer, most of the melons come up from Mississippi area. Can't think what he'd be doing. I know what I should be doing, I'll have to go."

"I'll look forward to going to the buffalo coat auction tomorrow. It should be fun."

"That's for sure."

"I think I'll go back early to St. Pierré, but I'd like to see what's at Rosa on the way." She put her hand in his. "Bye."

CHAPTER 14

Kathy changed her mind about going straight back to the motel once she was again on the road. Instead she turned to the right after passing Rosa, to go along by the Rat River. It was a beautiful evening, very cool and she only set off again when she felt hungry.

After driving a couple of miles along a grit road, she saw a bonfire burning brightly in a farmyard, where a family party was in progress. Dusk and evening shadows lent a dramatic quality to the scene.

That looks fun, she thought, I'd love to have a photo of that. So when a young man with two children, collecting sticks for the fire, waved to her, the camera clicked, she had her photograph.

"Come on down," he called. She went to meet them.

"Is it a party?" she asked.

"It's a wiener-roast," he told her. "You can come and join us if you like wieners and don't mind a bit of smoke."

"Thanks, I'd like to come."

"I'm Don," he held the gate open, and carrying his sticks, he and the children escorted her to where some people were sitting on a rug beside the fire.

"What's your name?" Don asked, throwing his sticks on the fire.

"Kathy, it's nice of you to ask me here."

He turned to a woman sitting on the rug. "Mother," he said, "This is Kathy. She was taking a photo and I asked her to come in."

"I'm Anna," she said, shaking Kathy's hand. "We have a wiener-roast for family and friends in the evening at this time of year. A once a week get together, after most of the harvest's in."

"I just stopped to take a photo of the party, it looked so exciting. Something like this is lovely to see. I'm a student, on holiday from England."

Children jumped about with excitement and dogs barked.

"Here you are," Anna said, putting a green stick into Kathy's hand. "You'll need one of these to roast your wieners. It has to be a green stick, else it'd catch fire."

"I see, thanks. I'm lucky I was passing at the right time."

"Here's the wieners," Anna said, "you'll be hungry I expect. Do you want a drink?" She handed Kathy a Canada Dry, her favourite.

Some of the party already had wieners on their sticks and were roasting them. Don said, "Here, I'll show you what to do." He expertly pushed a sausage onto her stick. "Do you want a marshmallow on too?" he asked.

"Yes please, if that's what you do."

He put on a marshmallow, another sausage and another marshmallow before handing it to her. "Thanks," she said. While she was watching her supper roast and sizzle, Don explained the technique of the fire.

"It has to be burning brightly first, then wet grass is put on top to damp it down, that's called a smudge. It makes enough smoke to keep the mosquitoes away. They only sting about sundown anyway and they're all gone by September. I like September, it's beautiful, we call it the Indian Summer."

When their cooking was done, Don and Kathy found a seat on an old log. She sat happily gazing about her at all that was going on. Two dogs, their tongues lolling out, waited for a bit of Don's sausage. Some toddlers came over and rolled about. One rolled on top of Kathy and looking up with a gorgeous smile, said, "Hi."

"Hi," Kathy replied, taking the child on her knee.

Don looking down at the child said, "Hi there Joe, having a good time?" He sidled up to Don before scampering off with the dogs.

The children ran barefoot on the grass, some in little cowboy hats. Kathy had taken her shoes off too. She liked to feel the grass under her feet, conscious again of a quiet sense entering her soul. A perfect way to end a summer evening, she thought.

"You're from England then?" Don said. "I'm glad you came in, we don't get many tourists along here. It makes a change to have someone new to talk to. We have to make our own fun mostly. There's always plenty to do on the farm, but my friends and I go to town at the weekends."

"I expect you look forward to that. I'm a student, so I've always got company in term time. I've had a great time over here though."

Don looked across at the little ones now riding a docile grey pony. It had to be docile as five little children were on its back at one time. They rode bareback; sticking their small toes into the pony's flanks, they were off.

"Don't they put a saddle on?" Kathy asked.

"No, Dad says it's safer without one. If they had a saddle and didn't belt it up properly it would slip and be dangerous. They don't come to any harm. I used to ride that way, still do sometimes."

Dew was beginning to settle on the grass and the sun was going down. Kathy put her shoes on. "I'll remember this evening when I get home on Saturday. Thanks for asking me in and giving me a lovely memory of Canada," she said to Don.

"My pleasure," he said, "I'll walk up to the gate with you."

The children were leaving with their parents. Kathy said, "Goodbye," to Anna and the others who were collecting paper cups and plates to throw onto the fire.

As she walked to the gate with Don, she nearly trod on a frog in her path. Startled, it put its frog hands on its head for protection, a faint hope of survival. "I haven't seen one do that before, even though I'm a zoology student," she said.

Don picked it up and put it in a clump of grass saying, "The dogs eat them, that's one that got away." He opened the gate, "Safe journey home," he said, shaking her hand.

She drove away feeling the gentle kindness of the family go with her.

CHAPTER 15

Good, I didn't sleep in, Kathy said to herself, as she jumped out of bed the next morning. She wanted to go out in time to see the mist rising from the surface of a small lake she'd seen just out of St. Pierré. She'd told Jacqui where she was going and asked her to tell anyone wanting her, where she was going, that she wouldn't be long, and to leave a message.

It's beautiful here, she thought, as she sat on a piece of shale near the water's edge and listened to the ducks quacking and the frogs croaking. Shafts of golden sunlight fell on a field nearby and made bright green and yellow patches on the grass. For a while she stayed still to watch a bright emerald tree-frog sitting on a sapling near her, its little black beady eyes gazing at her. Reeds grew in little clumps at the water's edge and a large blue-grey heron, startled her as it spread its wings and flew away. She watched it disappear out of sight.

Kathy had wanted this little time of peace. Everything had been so hectic since she'd arrived in Canada, nothing seemed certain anymore. Albert would come for her later in the day to take her to the buffalo coat auction. All reality seemed bound up with him, she only felt complete when he was with her.

She was thinking of getting up to go, the mist having cleared, when she heard someone coming along the track. Maybe a fisherman, but then she recognised Albert's walk. She let him come up beside her before turning to greet him. He sat down beside her and put his arm around her.

"I knew it was you Albert, I know your walk."

"I reckon you did."

"I'm always glad to see you." She gave him a little hug.

"I wanted to tell you I may be a bit late calling for you this afternoon. I'm on my way to Kleefield and I could get held up, I didn't want you to think I wasn't coming."

"I didn't think you'd stand any girl up Albert."

He looked at her quizzically. "Especially not you. How come you're fishing for compliments this morning?"

58

"Well, I thought maybe my being with Tim on Monday night might have put you off a bit. I was just fishing for reassurance that's all."

"Oh that's all! If you love you trust."

"You do love me?"

"You should know that my now Kathy."

"It's nice to hear you say so."

"I love you," he said, giving her a kiss. "You either believe it or not, which is it?"

"I believe you."

"You love me too?" he asked.

"I really do. I can't help myself. I'm sorry. I'm all right now," she said.

He gave her a quick cuddle. "That's good, I can't stay long though."

They sat quietly for a few minutes, then Kathy said, "Last night I walked along the Rat River. I don't mean in the middle of the night, the evening. It was so warm I waded in the water and when I got out my legs had big black leeches hanging all over them. It was horrible. I had no idea they were there, I didn't feel a thing. Do you know what else I saw?"

"No, I guess not."

"I saw the footprints of a baby in the sand along the riverbank. They were so small and perfect that I wished I could dig them up, dry them out and take them home with me for a work of art."

Albert was quiet. She looked at him. "They were baby bear's footprints," he said solemnly. "If the mother had seen you, you wouldn't be here to tell the tale."

"I didn't think there'd be bears there."

"There are. There are hundreds of black bear incidents every year in this part of the country. That's what I keep trying to tell you. You shouldn't go wandering around all over the place on your own. Your mother and father shouldn't have let you come alone."

"I realise now I've been taking risks."

"I don't suppose anyone thought you'd be so adventurous," he said giving her a big hug, "but your dad might have guessed. The trouble is you're going into places where animals hide out. All round

59

here there are skunks, some of them with rabies, there's bobcats, moose and further down there's lynx and the odd cougar, so you see what I mean. They're probably sitting out there watching you. The timber-wolves are less likely to hurt you than some others, but as you know, they're out there too. A moose can trample you to death."

Kathy listened, a bit cast down. "I'm sorry," she said.

"It's okay, you can't be expected to know all that," he said reassuringly. "You can't swim in these lakes either, there's bacteria in the water that will make your ears sore, unless you wear earplugs. If you want to swim at St. Malo you should get earplugs from the chemist in St. Pierré."

"All right, I'll be more careful. I want to tell you something else. I was standing picking berries over there, by the Rat River and I stepped backwards onto a little path and bumped into a white-tailed deer. It didn't see me in the bushes and I didn't see it coming along the path. I got back off the path to let it pass and it looked at me as if to say, "You know, you should look where you're going." We both got a fright and stared at one another wondering what had hit us."

"I hope you apologized then." Albert shook his head. "That's not usual for a deer to do that, they're very timid, as you know."

"I watched it go, it was so special."

"Like you," he said, standing up. "Coming?"

"Coming," she replied, offering him her hand to pull her up. "It's lovely here and to think I might have been in a black bear's tummy."

"We won't go into that, if you don't mind."

"I went to a wiener roast last night too. I'll tell you about it when you've got more time."

CHAPTER 16

Kathy and Albert were sifting through a pile of buffalo coats, trying to make up their minds which ones to bid for, when they found a very large one.

"Oh boy! Look at this one," Albert said, "I reckon it could take the two of us. He must have been a good size, the guy who wore this one."

"Let's try it on."

"Okay." Albert put an arm into one sleeve and Kathy an arm into the other, her head poking out of the collar as she tried to button it up.

"Stop wriggling Albert," she ordered, "Albert, I can't do up the buttons."

Just then John appeared. "Hi Albert, does the girl come with the coat?"

They got themselves out of it and John, pretending to be shocked, asked, "Are you intending buying that coat?"

"Sure," Albert said, "two for the price of one."

"You had a pretty bad experience Kathy. Albert told me about how you both escaped from the bushfire. That must have been scary stuff."

"It was, Albert saved my life, coming along when he did. I don't know what would have happened if he hadn't."

"I guess not. Albert's your man, fast worker, expert guide. I'm glad it's had a happy ending."

Albert put an arm round Kathy, John smiled. "I'll be off then you guys. I'll see you at the meeting tonight Albert. See you Kathy."

"Sure thing John." To Kathy he said, "The meeting's about Indian Affairs."

Half an hour later they each owned a buffalo coat, having paid thirty-five dollars each for them.

"They soon sold that lot," Kathy remarked as they stowed them away in the boot of the car. "Let's go to the Hudson's Bay coffee shop. It's my turn to pay, it's cheesecake for me," she added, "I can't get enough of it."

Seated at the counter, Kathy asked, "Will you be wearing you buffalo coat this winter?"

"That's what I had in mind, it can be really cold here, fifty or more below zero at times. Winnipeg and Moscow are the two coldest cities on earth, did you know that?"

"Yes I did, but not having experienced it myself, it's unimaginable. Not much wonder then, that people wore buffalo coats."

"Have you seen those giant statues of buffalo on the top of the steps of the Legislative Assembly building over there?" Albert asked.

"No, I know there's a buffalo on the Manitoba coat of arms though."

"We could go over to see them if you like, then we could sit in the park."

"I'd like that," Kathy said. "There were some buffalo bones in the bush were Jake lives. His little brother took me to see them, but he didn't know what they were."

"Tolstoi was about the limit of their range, too swampy further to the east towards Ontario."

"Manitoba's quite a place," Kathy said, "swamps, permafrost about fourteen feet down, and permafires that break out in hot weather. It's what could be called untamed, that's what I like about it."

"Untameable much of it."

"What do people do out in the country in winter?"

"Get jobs indoors. On the farms life goes on, it's tough, but people get used to the cold, younger ones go skating."

"Do you go skating?"

"Sure I do, everyone who can, skates. As soon as a child can walk they're given a pair of skates. I remember one night, a year or two ago, skating down a frozen river in the moonlight, on my own and feeling like a spaceman. The silence, the stillness and the stars. Just every now and then a tree would pop with the frost." He looked at Kathy. "Sorry," he said, "I got a bit carried away there, but winter can be magic, can't it?"

"What do you mean, trees pop?"

"When it's about forty below, any sap in the trees freezes and the tree breaks open with a pop. Like a gun going off."

"That so?"

"Sure. Winter's great, a lot of fun, if you're prepared for it. At one time Native Americans thought that a display of the Northern Lights was a dance of the spirits of the dead. That's great to see across the sky."

They were sitting under the shade of a tree in the park, when Kathy asked, "Do you know any funny animal stories?"

"Not many. There was a parrot at the Assiniborne Park Zoo in Winnipeg who called out to everyone going past, 'Have a nice day'."

"Birds can be very funny. I know of some seagulls at home who sat and watched TV through a window," Kathy said.

"Some bored gorillas were given a telly to watch. They liked cartoons, but the keeper turned it off if they watched it for too long. Zoos can't be heaven for all creatures, however hard we try."

"It's okay for the endangered species, but who really wants them locked up either."

CHAPTER 17

Albert rang Kathy just after breakfast the following morning. "I'm going to Grunthal, I could pick you up in about twenty minutes if you like."

"Yes I'll come. I'll be ready." She was pleased to get an unexpected trip out.

When on the road Albert explained the situation. "The hunting season starts next week. Some farmers don't want hunting on their land, but they can't stop it unless they put up notices, 'No Hunting on this Land'. I've got some notices for farmers to put up and some other things to do. I can pick you up in about an hour from the one and only café. Okay?"

When Albert had gone, Kathy looked down the almost deserted main street of the village. One or two trucks moved along as farming families collected supplies, but it was all very quiet. She had a look round a five-cent shop and a fabric shop, then bought some Canada geese table-mats from another before going to the café.

On asking the assistant what cold drinks she had, the girl replied, "7-Up, Canada Dry, Root Beer, Coke or Swamp Water."

"Swamp water?" Kathy said, "What's that?"

"A mix of them all," she was told.

"I'll try that. I can always then say I've tasted swamp water, that can be a talking point when I get home."

When Albert came in he turned down the swamp water in favour of Coke. Back on the road he chose a different route out of Grunthal. They'd only gone a short distance, when they were held up by some garter-snakes crossing the road. "I don't like to run over them, enough of them get killed on the road as it is. When they go on a hibernating trek, there are hundreds of them crossing this road."

"Phew! What a smell," Kathy said, a little further on.

"Hold your nose," Albert warned, "there's a dead skunk on the road."

"I don't think I've smelt a worse smell," Kathy declared.

Albert had quickly shut the car windows, but the smell still got inside. "It's worse if you run over one, the car smells awful for days," he said. "Now I'm beginning to think I shouldn't have come this way."

A few hundred yards further on they saw a red truck parked ahead and there seemed to be some sort of commotion going on. Kathy recognized the English students, girls she'd seen in the café at St. Pierré a few days earlier. They were being harassed by a young man who had them pinned down between the truck, a barbed wire fence and himself.

"That's Jake," Kathy said anxiously.

"What's he doing?" Albert said, driving down the side of the truck, though there was little room to manoeuvre. Jake was swinging a dead skunk around in front of the girls. The smell was overpowering.

"Is that Jake who locked you in the stable?"

"Yes."

"He must be drunk or crazy." Albert stopped the car just ahead of Jake's truck and put on a heavy-duty pair of gloves. "I'll go behind him and grab the skunk, while you distract him Kathy. He's got a gun on the seat of the truck. Make sure you get his registration number."

"Hi Jake," Kathy called.

He got a shock on seeing her there; the girls took the chance to run away.

"You locked me in the stable," Kathy shouted, "and you didn't come back and let me out. How was that?"

Albert had crept up behind Jake and grabbed the skunk. Flinging it as far as he could into the field, he shouted at Jake, "I could just sling you after it, get out of here before I change my mind."

As the dust cloud rose behind Jake they drove off.

"We'd better get out of his way fast," Albert said, "I think he's drunk. We'll be back on the highway in a few minutes."

However, a truck coming in the opposite direction slowed them down and Jake caught up with them. "Put your head down Kathy," Albert warned. She did what he told her, holding her breath, wondering what would happen next. Fortunately the occupants of the other truck were forestry workers. One grabbed Jake's gun.

Handing it to his mate he shouted at Jake, "I'll hand your gun into the police station and tell them it's yours."

"We'll corroborate your story," Albert said. Jake, knowing he was beaten, shot away ahead of the other truck.

"That was all a bit nasty. Hope you weren't too scared Kathy."

"No, it's all right. I'm getting used to that sort of thing happening. I won't be able to stand the peaceful life when I get home."

"It was sure a bit wild." Tentatively he asked, "Would you like to go out for a meal this evening as it's your last day tomorrow down here?"

"I'd like that very much," she said, trying not to show how she felt, she was hardly able to cope with the thought of leaving him behind. Albert seemed to be concentrating on the road ahead.

CHAPTER 18

When Mum first went out with Dad, did she feel as I do, about Albert? Kathy wondered. Relationships, it's not possible for outsiders to know what really exists between two people, the deep understanding and flashes of insight that flow from one to the other.

Albert has stood up to race prejudice and gone out into an alien community and conquered it, while things just seem to happen to me. I came to Canada, that was me doing something and yet that's turned out a bit wild, but I wouldn't have missed it for anything.

She sat eating a plum, then threw the stone into the water. The ripples spread out into a large circle; like my life, she thought, one little incident and it had set imperceptible events in motion. Here beside the Red River, drawn to it like a magnet, she mused over the powerful forces that had taken hold of her.

Aunt Ida, what had happened to her, she still hadn't found out. Now she herself was going to have to make some important choices. I would never make things hard for Albert. I would do my best to take care of him, learn about his people, and perhaps come back to Canada and live my life here. She thought of the Bible story of Ruth and Naomi, Ruth saying; 'Wither thou goest, I will go; and where thou lodgest, I will lodge; thy people shall be my people.' Is that how it must be for me? Is that to be my destiny? Was Albert at that point too, standing alone somewhere, not far away, making his choices.

At least she was doing what he told her to do. This wasn't a lonely dangerous place she'd come to, but the outskirts of Winnipeg. She wanted to buy herself a new pair of shoes and get her hair styled, before meeting Albert. She knew he would appreciate that.

It started to rain and the sky had suddenly become dark. The wind got up and the clouds whirled around. She got to the car as the first hailstones danced about her feet. Just another prairie thunderstorm.

Before Albert left her at St. Pierré, Kathy had said she hoped to get a hair-do in the afternoon. To her surprise he said, "I'll tell you where you could get one if you'd like to go. My sister Mary has a holiday job in a hair salon. I could give her a ring to tell her you're coming."

Kathy was delighted at the prospect of a meeting with Albert's sister. Now it was time to go. A short drive and a few minutes later she found herself being introduced to a small girl with long black hair. Not a bit like Albert, she thought, shaking her hand.

Mary smiled, "Pleased to meet you," she said, escorting her to a chair.

"I'm glad Albert suggested my coming to you. As you probably heard, Albert and I had a very dramatic start to our friendship."

"I know, but Albert made light of it when he told me," Mary said.

"It was pretty scary," Kathy replied.

"I couldn't think what Albert was on about when he phoned. It was a surprise. I knew he was seeing someone though." She laughed, "I asked him if he'd been bitten by the love-bug, but he said that the symptoms didn't always show up right away, to ask him next week."

Kathy smiled, "I guess there's some truth in that. Of course I'll be gone next week, back home to England, and I won't find it easy to say goodbye to Albert."

"Well I'll have to do my best to make you look very glamorous, not that it will be difficult," she assured Kathy confidently.

"The dust has got into my hair and the sun's dried it out." It seemed strange to have Albert's sister arranging her hair, but she felt it had helped to break down barriers that might have existed. They felt comfortable with one another.

On leaving, Kathy turned to Mary, "Thanks I like my hair. I hope I see you again."

"Me too," she said warmly. "I hope you have a good journey home."

CHAPTER 19

Albert had chosen a small quiet restaurant for their meal together. There was a bit of tension between them, showing in Kathy's first remark.

"I've had a pretty eventful holiday, you must admit," she said wryly.

Albert lifted his glass. "Here's to our future Kathy. A long life and a happy one."

"I'll drink to that," she said raising her glass, "to our future. It seems ages since I first saw you in St. Pierré. It was about the most embarrassing thing that ever happened to me. When you caught me making an assessment of you, I didn't know where to put myself."

"Oh boy, was that what it was?"

"It was your voice that first attracted me, I had to look round and I was smitten right away."

"I reckon we both were, but it took a bushfire to get us together and I'll never be the same again. John said he knew right away where it would lead, when we met again. When I first saw you I thought, now, I couldn't get that lucky and put the idea out of my mind."

"Albert that's nice, but I thought maybe you shovelled young women off the ground when they fell at your feet."

"Oh sure I do."

"And John's your side-kick, is he? I should have got more out of Mary."

"She's always been my ally. How did you two get along? I like the hair-do."

"Thanks, I like it. Your sister's nice. I liked her a lot."

"I'm glad, she's kind-hearted, got a great sense of humour."

"I had a sixth-sense about you Albert, from the start I felt we would mean a lot to each other. Perhaps a sixth-sense is just an educated guess?"

Albert paused. "No I don't think so. I figure it's something to take notice of. Animals have it. They have a strong sense that something's wrong and they get uneasy, don't they?"

"There's so much we don't know about animals. A lot of it is guesswork. Sometimes animals seem to think we're stupid."

"They've senses more powerful than ours."

"We'll be learning from them all our lives. You know Albert, I like you because you're Native American, not in spite of it."

"Oh thanks. That was a rapid change of subject, I hope you're not still referring to the animal kingdom?" he laughed.

"Seriously Albert, I meant what I said."

"I know, but I don't think being Native American's got anything to do with it. I think it's just that we have an empathy, and that can exist between any kind of people. Some go out trying to find someone right for them, and they can't."

"Like looking for a lost dream."

"Indian Reserves are dire places, but the place doesn't stop people falling in love. 'Aboriginal Rights', that's a big issue with us. Things are slowly improving though. At first it was difficult for white people to understand us, as Native Americans had no written language, only an oral history passed down from generation to generation. Each tribe had a different language, but they used sign-language, gestures with hands, arms and fingers."

"Not much wonder there were communication problems with white people. Anyway I know they didn't care much what happened to the Native Americans, it was all so cruel."

"We've learned to live together since then, in some kind of harmony." Albert took a sip of wine. "It's best to forgive and forget," he said.

"You know Neil Diamond's song, 'Cracklin Rosie'?"

"Sure."

"Do you know the story behind that song?"

"I do. 'Cracklin Rosie' is whiskey."

"Yes, consolation when there are no women left on the reserves in Northern Canada at the weekend, but he also said that a report about drunkenness among Native Americans, claimed they had a low alcohol tolerance level."

"I haven't seen that report, but for one reason or another, too many of them end up on the scrapheap. Education's been a problem, they've potential that's not being developed."

"I'm sure you're doing all you can. Albert, what about us? Where do we go from here?"

"Kathy, you know I love you. I'm working on something for us. Tomorrow I may have something interesting to tell you."

"May I guess."

"You wouldn't be able to."

"Maybe I can come back here for another holiday."

Albert took a small parcel from his pocket and placed it beside Kathy's plate. "For you," he said, "I hope you like it."

"Thank you," she said, leaning over to give him a kiss. Eagerly she unwrapped it. "It's lovely." She held a small carved canoe in her hand. "That will remind me of our trip down the river and the little carved Indian, well what can I say. Thanks so much, I love it. It will remind me of this evening too."

"Where are you going tomorrow?"

"To St. Malo in the morning, Tolstoi in the afternoon."

"What about tomorrow evening?"

"See how we feel, shall we?"

"If that's what you want. What about my coming up to you about half six?"

"Fine thanks."

"Shall we go now?" He rose slowly from the table. "I shan't know what to do with myself next week."

"Thanks for taking me out to so many places. I'll always remember the night you took me down the Red River in your canoe."

"Sometime we'll do it again."

"You and Manitoba, that's heaven to me."

"We'll see what we can do about it," he said.

CHAPTER 20

When Kathy went to St. Malo recreation park the following morning there were many groups of people and families already having a great time. The little lake in the clearing of the bush reflected the bright sunshine, as people in swimsuits, all colours of the rainbow, swam and splashed in the warm water. There were swings for the children and a little red slide at the water's edge where they slid shrieking with laughter into the water.

There were picnic tables and barbecues, supplied with plenty of wood for those who wanted to do their own cooking. Kathy took off her shoes to walk barefoot on the cool grass. At a chalet where hotdogs and ice-cream were being sold, she bought a hotdog and sat down at one of the picnic tables.

Some people were busy cooking and this, along with the aromatic smell of wood smoke, Kathy found intoxicating. Looking around, she felt someone here just might have known her Aunt Ida; she'd make some inquiries. An opportunity presented itself when a girl about her own age sat down at her table.

"Hi!" the girl said, "Do you live around here?"

"I'm from England, this is the last day of my holiday."

"Oh that's a shame. Have you had a good time?"

"Yes, I love Canada, maybe I'll come back another time."

"I'm Emily," the girl said. "My mum and gran are over there, sitting under the trees in the shade."

"Do you come here often?"

"Once a week in the summer."

"I wonder if you could help me?" Kathy took the photo of her aunt out of her handbag. Handing it to Emily she asked, "Do you know who she is? She once lived round here somewhere."

Emily looked at the photo. "No I haven't seen her anywhere, but maybe my mum or gran might have. They've lived here all their lives. Shall we go and ask them?"

They looked up when Emily and Kathy approached. She held out the old photograph. "Emily thought you might have known this woman. She is a great-aunt of mine who lived round here at one time."

Emily's gran took one look at it and said, "I know who that is, she once lived down by Tolstoi, but she died some time ago."

"Is that so?"

"That's for sure. I didn't know her well, just knew who she was. She was married to a farmer down there, lived out of Tolstoi, nearer to Gardenton. Do you know your way round there?"

"I'll be able to find the place. Thanks, I wanted to know what happened to her, that's all."

Kathy left them and went back to the car. That's the mystery solved then. Well I hardly expected to find her alive, but I'm sorry I didn't. She put on the radio. Bobby Bare was singing, 'Four Strong Winds' a melancholy song of winter. I wonder what winter's like out on the prairie? I can't imagine, she mused.

She had intended going straight to Tolstoi, but changed her mind, she wanted to see the Mennonite Historic Settlement of 1873 at Steinbach. On her way back through town she noticed Jake, standing by the water-melon stall where she'd seen the dodgy trader.

In the afternoon Kathy stopped at the Tolstoi store-come-Post Office, to post some cards home. As she needed stamps, she went inside to buy some. A washing-machine whirred away in the centre of the store. The merchandise as usual was piled up in every available space. The store owner-post mistress, poked the washing around in the machine with a stick, as steam rose gloriously upwards to mingle with the brooms and brushes hanging from the ceiling, while she chatted with the customers. Well, Kathy thought, I suppose if she wishes to do the washing in the middle of the store, why should it bother me. She looked around and bought two little Ukrainian silk scarves. Then the woman asked where Kathy'd come from.

"England," she said, "and I'd like stamps for my postcards please."

The woman looked uncertain, "U.K.," Kathy said, hoping to enlighten her.

"U.K.," the woman repeated, "to what commonwealth does that belong?"

Kathy replied, "England doesn't belong to anyone."

"Did at one time," the woman replied belligerently.

"No," Kathy said, "not since the Romans left." She decided to go before the woman could ask when the Romans left.

There was a little white-painted wooden school beside the road, a single rail track went through town, but there wasn't much to see. Better, she thought to go on to Gardenton, near the Canadian border. This time not a grit road, though the reason was not apparent until she saw on her left the most beautiful Ukrainian Greek Orthodox Church beside the road, among some trees. Kathy went over to read a plague. To commemorate the consecration of the first Ukrainian Greek Orthodox Church in Canada 1896 it said. It looks as if it's been transported from the Ukraine, complete with its lovely onion-shaped domes, she thought, before turning south where the gravel road began again.

It was a sultry afternoon, so she got out of the car and sat at the roadside, looking across to America, beyond a hayfield. A dramatic line of thunderheads, their white foam tops glistening in the sun, stretching for what she imagined to be a hundred miles or so, rose high into the summer sky. She was amazed how quickly the great white clouds grew in height as she watched them, like giant ice-cream cones, altering in shape all the time.

Not far away someone had planted gladiola and a tiny humming-bird, attracted by the brightly coloured flowers, hovered with its delicately curved beak, to penetrate the petals and gather the nectar from the base of the flower. She watched fascinated by its tiny whirring wings. It was then that she saw some small gravestones hidden among the grass. She went over to look and read on one stone, 'Ida Pawloski died 1951. Glen Pawloski died 1953'. So there she is, I did find her, Kathy said to herself. As she stood there in that peaceful place, making a link with the past, a caterpillar crawled across her foot. There was a smell of rain in the air and a soft breeze began to blow. Feeling it on her face, she whispered, "Goodbye Aunt Ida. Maybe I can come this way again." She went back to the car for her camera and took a photograph before leaving.

CHAPTER 21

I'll move on a bit and find a nice place to eat my lunch, Kathy thought. There was no one about. Canada seemed such a vast country, Manitoba, big enough to take the whole of the British Isles and then some. I'll feel strange when I'm back home, where distance are measured on a much smaller scale.

She hadn't gone far when she spotted an empty poplar-pole shack. I'll have to get a photo of that she thought and drove round the back of it to park the car under the shade of a tree.

"What a curious little house," she said out loud, as she stood looking at it, "it could be the house of the three bears." Inside there was a ladder type stair, not much of it left and pieces of crudely patterned lino on the floor.

As she stood looking round, to her surprise, she heard a car drive into the yard. Glancing quickly through a window, she saw a man get out of the car. Kathy recognized him as the man she'd puzzled about in Emerson the week before. What does he want here, she wondered. Feeling a bit scared, she dived into a little cupboard, hoping he wouldn't come in the house. She left the cupboard door ajar so that she could look and see what he would do.

As her car was round the back, he obviously didn't know she was there. He looked casually about the yard and then went over to an old pump beside a well. First he gave the handle a yank, then peered down into the well, finally he knelt down to have a closer look in. Immediately he stood up and ran to his car, making off at great speed, Kathy wondering what it was all about.

When all was quiet she went out and took a look in the well, but didn't notice anything odd. Then she saw a pocketbook lying on the ground. Obviously the man had dropped it, so she picked it up and took it into the house.

On opening it she found it contained some photos, credit cards and an envelope addressed to a Mr Larry Johnson, living in Winnipeg. She put the pocketbook on a windowsill, then remembered seeing a small zip holdall in the cupboard, where she'd been hiding. On opening it she discovered it contained a number of small plastic bags full of white powder. Drugs. Her heart started pounding.

Trying not to panic, she left the place in a hurry, forgetting the pocketbook. She drove down the road in the opposite direction from the one she'd come along earlier, thinking Larry had gone that way. She tried to compose herself, but felt very frightened. She turned off the road, down a track and found herself in a gravel pit. An excavator, for quarrying stone, stood beside a very high mound of gravel, obviously used for resurfacing the grit roads. She supposed the workmen had gone home for the weekend, as it was after three-thirty.

She sat listening to the local radio station, trying to calm herself and think where she'd seen the mystery man before. Then it suddenly dawned on her, the Winnipeg library, of course, he worked there. It still didn't explain what he was doing at the shack though.

She got out of the car and idly picked up one or two pieces of stone, strewn about by the excavator and noticed that many contained fossils of small sea creatures and shells. She gathered some up and put them into the car. Feeling more composed, she wondered what to do next, then decided to go back to St. Pierré. The thought made her feel sad, her holiday was coming to an end.

Just as she was about to start the car, she heard a news bulletin on the radio; there'd been a car-chase involving drugs and police at the border check point. It set her mind racing, now I have to make the right decision, she said to herself. First I must get the pocketbook. If I sit here and do nothing, Larry Johnson could be implicated in a crime he had nothing to do with, should the police turn up at the shack before I do.

Kathy wondered if it would be safe for her to go back there alone, and decided it would be wiser to phone and tell the police what she'd seen. Not knowing what lay ahead along the road, Kathy decided to climb a mound of grit, hoping to see from the top if there was a house nearby. Feeling safety conscious, she hung her camera round her neck, locked the car and put the key in her pocket before starting to climb up the high mound of stones.

She slithered and slid towards the top, trying not to scrape her knees on the sharp stones. At the top she set her feet firmly together

77

and gazed about. A sound down below caught her attention and her glance fell on a man getting out of a black van on a patch of grass behind a shed. I don't believe it, she said to herself, it's the melon man. He'd seen her and was making a dash for her, hoping no doubt to get her camera and film, confirming her opinion that drugs were involved in all this. Kathy realized she had no time to look for a house, to make a phone call now.

As she stopped to make her way down, she fell over to her right and found herself sliding on her back down towards the bush some few yards away. Apart from a cut on her leg she felt she was fortunate, as she could find cover in the bush and keeping parallel to the road, hopefully get some help.

Scrambling for cover she tried to make as little noise as possible, while getting well away from the melon man and the gravel pit. One of her shoes got stuck in a smelly black swamp. She remembered Albert's warning about swamps. Taking off the other shoe, she flung it after the first. It was cool and quiet among the trees, but her mind was set on her escape, no time to sit down.

Half an hour later she knew the melon man had lost track of her and she felt calmer though she was still in a desperate situation. She made her way to the road and peered up and down. To her amazement she found she was within a few yards of the shack and a police car was turning into the lane leading to the yard. She crossed the road and ran after it, then stood for a minute in the yard, wondering what to do. A policeman saw her and came towards her. Kathy felt very apprehensive when asked, "What do you want?"

"I was here about an hour ago," she told him. "Since then I heard on the radio, about a car chase involving drugs. I think I saw drugs in a bag in a cupboard in that shack," she explained.

"What were you doing here?"

"I came here to take some photos, but while I was here that man over there by the well, came up here and had a look round. I was in the house. He didn't know I was there as my car was round the back."

She looked over to where Larry Johnson was talking to another policeman by the well. "I knew I'd seen him before, but I couldn't remember where. I saw him look down the well and then he drove off in a hurry. When I went out to see what made him drive away so fast, I found his pocketbook lying on the ground."

"Where is it now?"

"In the shack."

"Why are you in such a mess?" he asked, looking at her with some concern. "Are you on holiday?"

"Yes, I'm a zoology student from England."

"Show me your passport please and your driving licence."

"Fine. I see you were over in the States at the weekend. Is there anyone round here who can vouch for you?"

"Well, Albert Thunder. We talk about zoology."

"I know Albert. Have you got his phone number?"

"I have it in my purse." She handed it to him, feeling anxious.

"Thanks Kathy," he said, "Don't upset yourself. I'll have a word with Albert."

She waited for him to make the call. Now what will Albert say, she wondered.

"It's okay, he's coming right over, asked if you were all right."

Things were becoming very complicated. Another officer and Larry Johnson were standing over a man's body that had been dragged from the well.

"I'm glad you came up and explained what was going on Kathy. Larry rushed off in a hurry to get us here when he saw the body, you'll understand," the policeman said.

Kathy shivered. "I didn't see the body in the well."

More police cars arrived, and Kathy was asked by an officer, to show him where the drugs were. She pointed out what she thought were drugs in the cupboard and the pocketbook she'd left on the windowsill.

"I wondered why Mr Johnson came here. I thought it must be something to do with drugs at first. I came up to take photos."

Larry's a water colour painter, thought he'd found a good subject, like you did," he replied, taking up the pocketbook.

They walked back to the others just as Albert and his brother drove up, looking perplexed. Kathy wished to be anywhere but where she was.

"Hi there," Albert said, looking at the streak of blood running down Kathy's leg and her very black feet. "Whatever's happened Kathy? How are you in such a mess?"

"I'm all right."

"Sorry to bring you out here Albert. This young lady says you know her, is that true?"

"Sure. What's happened?"

"Quite a lot. Kathy's not in trouble though." He turned to Robert. "Hi Robert, we've a body."

Albert's brother spotted the body on the ground by the well and went over. Albert and Kathy followed. The policeman enlightened them, saying, "Mr Johnson got us here. He found the body in the well. Do any of you know who the drowned man is?"

"It's Jake," Kathy and Albert said together, looking at the crumpled wet body on the ground.

"What's happened Kathy?" Albert's voice revealing his horror.

"I was being chased by the melon man. Jake was with him in Steinbach."

One officer looked at her closely, "Melon Man?" he repeated.

"Yes I thought he might be up to something when I saw him last week. I thought he was on the fiddle."

"Melons? What next? We've had just about everything else, we haven't had melons before."

"I took the man's photo. I have it in my camera," Kathy said shakily. "He got out of a van and chased me in the gravel pit, down there, that's why I'm in such a mess. I had to slide down a mound of gravel to get away from him, then I walked through the bush to hide from him. I lost a shoe in a little swamp," she said, looking at Albert with a woebegone face.

"Can I borrow the film? I'll let you have it back, we'll need it," the policeman explained.

"Sure." With hands too shaky, she tried to take it out.

"Give it to me," Albert said gently, "I'll take it out for you."

She turned to look at Jake's body, so strangely quiet. It was all too much for her, she started to cry. "I feel sick" she said, "and my car is still down at the gravel pit. When I found drugs in the shack I was scared and went off to find somewhere quiet. That's rather ironic isn't it?"

"Do you think the man's still there?" he asked.

"What colour was the van?" an officer asked.

"Black."

"We'll put out a call for it, a black van's easy to spot."

"Do you want to sit in my car Kathy?" Albert suggested, "While we sort things out here."

Turning to her, the officer in charge said, "You can go for your car if you like." To one of the men, he said, "Give her a lift in your car."

"Can I go too?" Albert asked, thinking Kathy looked too shocked to go alone.

"Thanks Albert," she said in a bleak voice.

There was no one there, no sign of the melon man or his van, when they arrived at the gravel pit. Kathy's car was still where she had left it, so Kathy and Albert drove back to the shack with their police escort.

"It's all right if you want to go now," they were told. "We won't need you anymore. Thanks for your help Kathy. It'll be a watertight case, if we get the man we're looking for."

"I hope so," she murmured.

"Thanks for coming back for my pocketbook," Larry Johnson said to Kathy, "a lot of people wouldn't have done that. It could have been very awkward for me."

Albert was very quiet, Robert looked serious, "You can't be called back from England for this," he said. "It's a shame you've had so much trouble. Don't worry about it anymore."

"I'll go home with Robert now," Albert explained and I'll come to St. Pierré this evening as we planned, okay?" He put his arm round her and gave her a hug. "Will you be able to drive now?" he asked.

"Sure, I'll be all right," she said reassuringly.

There was an eeriness about the place, Kathy thought, as she left the scene. She felt very gloomy and had the impression that Albert wasn't very pleased. He's always risking his neck for me, she thought. Her relationship with Albert couldn't stand much more of this sort of thing, it would probably already be finished.

Oh why did I ever come to Canada on my own? I don't know how I'm going to face Albert tonight, she grumbled. All she wanted to do was get out of the country and never come back. Things she thought had just gone from bad to worse. I'll leave the motel and spend the night somewhere else where Albert can't find me. What kind of a relationship is it anyway? If I can't manage things on my own, I'm not having him doing everything for me. I feel I'm in disgrace. It all started with this stupid car breaking down. I've made a complete fool of myself. I can't believe it's all happened.

She wrote a note to Albert and left it with Jacqui. After packing her case, she sat in the bedroom trying to calm herself. Albert will realize how I feel, but I'm not at all sure what he thinks of me. I've just turned out to be a load of trouble for him.

She began to feel ill. Going down to the lounge, she sat with a cup of coffee. She'd had a shower, getting rid of the remnants of the swamp mud. What smelly stuff. That was a grand finale, I must say she thought. She remembered what John Lennon had said, 'Life is what happens to you while you are busy planning something else'. How true, she mused.

As she sat wondering, she lost track of time. Just as she was putting her case in the car, Albert drove up. He looked surprised when he realized what she was doing.

"Why are you going Kathy? I thought we were to spend the evening together."

"I can't stand any more Albert, I just want to go home."

Albert just stood looking at her.

"You can't help but be fed up with me, after all I've done. What's left for me here? I've got to go." She leaned against the car, her head down.

"Okay, but let me tell you something first, before you go," he insisted.

"Well," she said quietly, without looking up. "What do you want to say?"

"I told you last night, I might have something to tell you, that would make you happy."

"I don't know of anything that can make me happy now. Can't you see Albert, it's just not on. I've made a complete ass of myself. I even feel I've been trespassing on your ground. Manitoba, it's your space, I'm an alien."

Albert said nothing, he only hoped she'd calm the tangled state of her mind and listen to reason.

After a few minutes silence, she said. "All right, what did you want to tell me?"

"Only that I'll be going over to England in about three weeks time. I've got a six week job, with a film company in Salt Lake City. I'm to take wildlife film and show it in cinemas across Britain, in aid of conservation. I'll also be giving talks on Ancient Native American Trails."

Katy looked at him, as if he had suddenly said he was going to the moon.

"You see," he said, "I didn't know till today that I was definitely going. You told me the other day that if you didn't see me again when you went back home, you'd be lonely for the rest of your life. Well I feel the same way about you."

Kathy had been taking it all in. "That's amazing Albert, what can I say?"

He bent down and kissed her. Putting his arm around her, he said, "See I said it might all work out. Could we go in for a while and talk? Then maybe have a walk out afterwards?"

They sat in the lounge and Jacqui put her head round the door. "More coffee?" she asked.

Kathy nodded. "Yes please."

"I figured you'd be wanting some," she said knowingly, turning towards the kitchen.

"She's kind, isn't she Albert?"

"She is that." He took her hand. "That was all a terribly harrowing experience, Jake being found drowned."

"What a shame, his family were nice to me."

Albert nodded. "Terrible, I wonder how it happened? If he was involved with drugs it's not surprising he was acting like he was crazy, being involved with criminals too."

Kathy agreed. "It does look as if he was."

83

"There's lots of drugs around," Albert said, "but let's change the subject, I'll be able to see Slimridge, I'll love that, Windsor Great Park and the New Forest; that isn't new, when I go to England."

"That will be wonderful, I'm so glad Albert, I love you so much."

They sat quietly thinking about all that had happened, then Kathy said, "I'm lucky to have got out of all that trouble, it all happened so fast."

"Shall we go out now?"

"Yes I'd like that," she said, putting her hand in his.

They walked a little distance along the road. "I'll so look forward to your coming over to England," she said.

"There will be four of us going, two for the north of England, two for the south. I'll be working from Bristol."

"It must have been meant to be," Kathy said, "do you believe in destiny?"

"I think we make our own, but sometimes we get a bit of help."

"I don't know what part the mosquitoes play, but I'd like to get out of their way for a bit."

"Okay. They're a nuisance, but by September they're all gone."

There was a little white church in a patch of grass a few yards from the road. The lights were on. "Let's go in there and sit down," Kathy suggested. They took a seat in the shadow at the back. "It's beautiful in here isn't it," she whispered. "I go to an evangelical church in Cardiff. Lots of students go, because the Welsh people love to sing in choirs."

"I've heard they do."

"Do you know they were the first people to arrive in the Salt Lake City area; before the Mormons got there?"

"No I didn't."

"They started the singing tradition, that still goes on. This is a catholic church, you'd expect that in St. Pierré, where most people are French Canadians, but Manitoba is the home of the Native American spirit Manitou, isn't it?" she whispered.

"That's so."

A few minutes later she said, "I found my Aunt Ida's grave near Gardenton, this afternoon."

"Is that so?"

"She died in 1951."

"That's a shame, you didn't get to speak to her."

"It doesn't matter. I didn't really think I'd see her."

"Do you feel better?" Albert asked, stroking her head.

"Yes, I feel all right thanks, are you?"

"Yes. Do you love me?"

"You know I do."

"I love you too."

"I love you so much Albert. To me you are like a symphony, what you look like, your voice, what I read in your eyes. You're like music, to me."

"That's a lovely thing to say." He held her close. "I want to ask you something before you go home Kathy. Could you think about marrying me?"

She looked up at him and said gently, "I don't need to think Albert, I know. It won't be 'Farewell to the Red River Valley' more like 'Cathy Come Home', but for me it's not a tragedy because you took care of me."

"I wouldn't let anything happen to you Kathy. It's no half measures with me. I won't let you down."

"Will the Great Spirit Manitou give us a blessing? I'd like that Albert."

"Sure."

They sat quietly together for a few minutes, before walking out of the church and back to the motel. Albert said, "I'd like to go for a swim. I thought about it this morning before all the trouble started. How about you?"

"Could we?"

"For sure we could."

"Where can we go?"

"There's a pool in the river about a mile away. I've been there before and there's no mosquitoes."

"Okay I'll go and get a couple of towels. I won't be a minute."

A short drive took them to a little pool in the river, sheltered by trees and the bush. "What a lovely place, all to ourselves," Kathy exclaimed.

Albert, standing behind her, put his hands on her shoulders, "It won't be dark for an hour, so we've got plenty of time. Okay?"

"I'm happy."

"Well let's jump in" he said. Albert, to Kathy's astonishment, stripped off all his clothes, jumped into the water and swam a little way out.

Kathy hesitate a moment, then threw her clothes off and followed him in. "The water's still warm," she said, ducking below the surface and coming up just beside him. She pushed her hair back laughing. "I'm glad you thought of this," she said, holding out her hand to him. He pulled her towards him and gave her a kiss. "You're a lovely girl Kathy," he said.

She looked lovingly into his eyes, "I'll always think you're drop dead gorgeous Albert. I can't believe I'm so lucky to have you, and you always surprise me with the things you do." She swam to a large stone and sat on it.

"You look like a mermaid sitting there," Albert called out. All you need is a comb. All mermaids comb their hair, don't they?" He came to where she sat. "I haven't got a fish's tail," she said, splashing him with her feet. "Maybe if I stay in the water long enough I'll grow one." She slipped down into the water, "It's warmer in here," she added, "and anyway you're in here."

They laughed and splashed each other in a waterfall as their troubles left them and drifted down the river. They came out of the pool holding hands. Kathy grabbed a towel and started to dry her hair, "I feel all glowing warm all over," she said, "Are you?"

"That's for sure. I know how to stay warm," he said tenderly.

"So do I, but have you set your alarm clock?"

"I didn't bring it."

"Neither did I."

He moved over to her and they held each other.

"We can't stay here any longer," he said, "too much wildlife. Let's go back to the motel, shall we? I just want you so much."

After saying goodbye, Kathy returned to her room again and opened the window to let in the sounds of the night. I've learned a lot since I came here, she thought, sitting down on the bed, thinking of all that had happened in the last two weeks. The picture most vivid in her mind was of Albert, standing by a dried up ditch of twisted bulrushes and grass, of heat rising off the grit road, insects humming and chirping in the grass and of Albert gazing somewhere in the far distance, towards a thin blue line of trees.

Isobel King lives in Salisbury – 'Somewhere in the Far Distance' is her first book.

She spent five years in Manitoba, coming back to England in 1972, but she left her heart in Manitoba.

She has published a number of poems in magazines and anthologies.

Isobel has two grown up daughters, an 8 year old grandson, Duncan and a 5 month old granddaughter, Elizabeth.